The Magwitch Effect

The Magwitch Effect

Tony Lester

Introduction

Those readers of 'Great Expectations' who wondered how Abel Magwitch was able to send back money to England to create a gentleman can read the explanation in 'The Magwitch Story'. There it was shown how Amanda Jane, who had been transported previously, assisted Abel Magwitch. This book now tells the story from the viewpoint of Jane Alambard, who had also been transported and was a servant of Amanda Jane. It goes on to tell how Jane became Jane O'Brian and how the Magwitch Effect affected her and others.

Part one

The Magwitch Effect

Jane's Story

Never a lady

Chapter 1

Transported for Life

Goaded to the point where I completely lost my temper, I struck out at my tormentor. I caught him by surprise. He never expected plain, little, face-marked Jane to strike back. No one ever did. I never did, despite repeated provocations. The edge of my tray caught him on his jaw, opening a jagged cut that sprayed blood. He called out and fell back against the range catching his hand on the sharp black hot edge. This time he screamed and his scream made me drop the tray. They all gathered round Jem so I took the opportunity to run, but Ann, the maid I shared a room with, held me fast.

I was brought to the butler who was more upset at Jem's uniform being bloodied than Jem's injuries. He listened as he heard how a mild, gentle kitchen maid had suddenly gone mad and attacked Jem Akenhead, one of the house's footmen. No-one explained how I had been bullied ever since I joined Squire Roger's household, how I had suffered endless provocation due to the fact that my face was not "right". I had seen similar behaviour amongst the animals at the farm where I was born. Any animal that was different was liable to be turned upon by the others. I had thought that human beings would be different. I was wrong. So, having been born with a lop-sided face and then contracting smallpox, my face was certainly not my fortune. I had been told that my great grandmother had been burned as a witch. Maybe all her descendants were destined for a similar grisly fate. My mother, God rest her soul, was dead, and most likely at the hands of some drunken ruffian. I never really knew what happened to her.

The butler decided that I should be brought before the magistrate, who just happened to be Squire Rogers. He decided that I had attempted to murder Jem so had me sent to the Quarter Sessions. There I was found guilty and told by a Judge that I, Jane Alambard, was a wicked depraved creature who had set myself up against a good God who had seen fit to make sure that, through giving me a distorted face, I was fit to serve with the lowest part of society. He said that he would normally have sentenced me to hang, but he wanted to give me a chance to redeem myself, so was ordering me to be transported for life to New South Wales.

To be honest, I thought that he meant that I was to be sent to some part of Wales, and it was not until I joined the others in the gaol that had also been sentenced that I found out that I was to be transported. Even then what this meant did not mean very much until I was taken with the others and placed on a boat. Having never seen the sea, nor a port for that matter, I did not even know from whence I departed England.

At that time I had no idea how one man, Abel Magwitch, was to dominate my life. The story of how he was also transported to New South Wales and how he made a gentleman of a young blacksmith, Pip Pirrip, is told elsewhere. You can also read how my mistress in Sydney assisted him, and how I was involved in that, to some extent, despite my worries about the authorities. Pip's arrival and his later adventures with John Adam can also be read in another book, as can his later involvement with Estella. This, however, is an account where I tell the story from my side, and shows how Magwitch's existence had a lasting impact upon us all. I am writing it here in this home where they all think that I am waiting for my daughter to visit me. I'm not. I'm waiting for a more important visitor: death.

But to return to my journey on the boat to Australia; it was certainly no more arduous than many others endured, and the privations that I suffered were not that severe. I was accepted by all as yet another unfortunate, and indeed, enjoyed more kindness from these criminals than had ever been my lot up to this time. I was young and sturdy, could turn my hand to all those kinds of skills that a young woman brought up on a farm might have, so I thought, as we moved nearer to New South Wales, that I might get a good billet. On the boat the men avoided me, preferring more attractive females. This did not bother me; it was what I had always experienced in my short life.

Because we were the latest in a series of ships that had made this journey, our captain had learned from previous trips that it was best to deal with us with a certain amount of compassion. I think he was also paid more if more convicts were delivered in a fairly healthy state as the colony wanted hands that could work. Half-starved unfit men and women were not so acceptable. So our food was tolerable. I learned from the seamen that worked the ship that they called it a boat, and that the food that we got was just about what they were used to. In time, as we sailed on, and called in at various places our food changed. It became more varied. I was popular as I generally avoided too much liquor, so when any was served out I gave mine to someone else. Recognising the value of vegetables, I often traded any rum for an extra amount of vegetables where I could. The main problem was that the food was so monotonous.

We also suffered from boredom. As someone who could use a needle I never lacked something to do. Whether it was sewing up an old jacket or patching a shirt. No one had any clothes that were new, not even the crew. Even the ship's master wore a well-worn coat, and as for his hat, I never saw him wear anything except a battered thing that served him well enough but would have been abandoned long ago by any gentleman ashore.

Our surgeon served on board because he had lately been with the army, and was tired of sawing off limbs that had been mutilated by the enemy. I never really found out from him who the enemy were. I suppose it was the French. Apart from his skill as a surgeon he was a talented man and could play many a good tune upon what I thought was a whistle of some sort. It had a much grander name, but I have forgotten it. He spoke several languages. The first time I heard him jabbering in a foreign lingo was at our first port of call. It astonished me. Poor simple girl that I was, I thought everyone spoke English.

I said as much and got laughed at for my pains. The surgeon, who was really a kindly man, and seeing my distress, tried to divert me my lending me a book to read. Then, seeing that I was struggling with the words, he got his assistant to give me some instruction. To everyone's astonishment, not least of all mine, I came on handsomely. It seemed I had a talent for reading, and where others really struggled with books and then gave up, I found it so easy that I rapidly became an avid reader, and positively devoured them when I could.

As we got further and further from England we began to experience all sorts of extreme weather. The extreme heat occasionally made most of the convicts very fractious leading to many arguments as a result. There were some assaults too which led to the perpetrators being put back into irons that had been struck off as we set out. I was amazed at how often we had farm animals aboard, but quickly came to realise that they both provided food and drink as they would on a farm, and were to be used in the new country where we had been sent. I could not imagine a country without sheep and cows and pigs. When the crew spoke of the strange animals that we would find I thought that they were making mock of me.

One day we were all informed that we would shortly, God willing, be at our destination. We were told to make ourselves as presentable as we could for we would virtually be slaves to be chosen as such, to labour in whatever capacity our new masters and mistresses would choose. Unfortunately, my appearance meant that when we did arrive I was not chosen to be a servant, as many women were. I was nearly taken on, but rejected when my new master and mistress heard of my crime. They said that, having children, they could not risk having me. My face and my attack upon my tormentor spoiled my chances. So instead I was sent to Parramatta where I languished, as they had not at that time constructed the factory.

Going up the muddy river to Parramatta was a time of great trial for me, for I was surrounded by all the worst sort of women, including some that had been employed in Sydney and had then forfeited the right to any sort of decent life because of their degradation. I determined to try to keep myself occupied and attempt to rise above this new state. To that end I not only continued to use my needle, but I also persuaded those in charge to allow me to teach others. Some were beyond help.

Their swearing and rough behaviour reminded me of some of those women who worked the land in England. Their behaviour did not shock me, but I saw, all too clearly what a poverty of existence was to be their lot in this country. Whenever I could, I read. There was always a Bible. I liked some of the stories that it contained.

Chapter 2

Rescued from Parramatta

It was something that I shall always remember. I was paraded in the moist heat with strange birds calling and the strange trees with their bark all hanging down in the red dust, to be looked over, along with the others, by a possible master. I stood there, listless in the sunshine. I looked up, scarcely interested, certain sure that I would be passed over once again, to see a young woman! She quickly passed down the line until she reached me.

"What is your name?"

"Jane, Jane Alambard. They call me plain Jane."

She then put a whole list of questions to me and, as she did so, I began to hope that my luck was going to change. I sensed that she was interested in employing me, and I presumed that I was wanted as a maid that might not interest the master or servants. Eventually she spoke to the foreman and then to my utter astonishment she came back and took my hand, clasping it in the friendliest manner.

"Jane. I am Amanda Jane. You are to come with me. I want you to be a general servant for my master, Mr Spackford, who has a house just outside Sydney."

I nodded to show my understanding. I could not trust myself to speak. She signed the necessary papers on behalf of her employer and we left. Before we did so several women came over to me to say farewell. All congratulated me on my good fortune. When I asked what they meant they all replied that anyone who escaped from Paramatta was to be congratulated. I thought that they knew something about my new master, but it was simply upon my escape that I was being congratulated.

On the journey to Mr Spackford's house, Amanda spent the whole journey instructing me as to my duties. She warned me to be most particular in accepting instructions only from her or Mr Spackford. I was to be most careful in my dealings with Maggie Senchal and Susan Abercrombie. She added that though she, like me, was a transported criminal, she was attempting to make something of her life and was not to be brought low by the likes of Maggie and Susan.

Chapter 3

A Marriage and a Death

I was most impressed with Mr Spackford's house when we arrived. It was surrounded by a shady veranda and had a dining room, a reception room, several bedrooms, a library, a kitchen, of course, and all sorts of out-houses. It was nothing near as grand as the Squire's house in England where I had been so unhappy, but I recognised that it was a substantial house in New South Wales where many lived in much less gracious dwellings. I met the other members of the household and quietly assumed my duties. I was mostly ignored by them, and that suited me completely. I even had a tiny whitewashed room of my own, a real luxury.

My duties were much more basic than those that I had to fulfil in England. Despite the house being so spacious and suitable for a gentleman, it was a working establishment where bread had to be baked each day, beer brewed, cream to be skimmed from the milk when the cows were milked, set aside, then churned into butter. We also made our own cheese, not so fine as that which I had enjoyed in England but tolerable.

I ate well too. We all did. Amanda Jane made all the servants eat together, and she inspected what we ate to make sure that it was wholesome. Despite this some of the others grumbled, saying that she only did this to get more work from us. And didn't we work? From first light there was always something that had to be done. As I said, I had a room of my own, but I was not allowed to spend that much time in it.

What little time I had to myself I spent reading for I had developed a thirst for books once I had managed to learn to read sufficiently well to get through them. My mistress encouraged me by lending me books.

It came as no surprise to me when we learned that Amanda Jane and Elias Spackford were to be wed. I had seen it coming for months. In this new country, things seemed to happen much quicker than they did in England. It was a quiet affair and within weeks it seemed so natural that we had a Mrs Spackford that I almost forgot the time when she was a housekeeper. She still went out collecting her herbs and on one occasion I saw her treat a sick horse that most had given up for dead. It was on its feet in a week and able to be saddled and ridden in no time. I ignored Maggie's mutterings about witch's brews. I had admired Amada when we first met and now I admired her even more. She had my loyalty that was shortly to be tested. Of my own history about witches I said nothing.

It was Maggie that found him. He had gone to have a sleep in the afternoon while Amanda rested on the bed in their room. It was astonishingly hot and humid and even I was half asleep, and instead of attending to my household duties I was dozing in the scullery, the coolest place that I could find. She screamed and ran along the veranda. Amanda Jane came out of her room looking hot and cross.

He was dead. Even I could see that. We had had deaths on the boat so I certainly knew what a dead man looked like. Maggie would not be quiet and soon Susan was crying too. They carried on as if it was their husband as had died. The doctor said it was probably a snake. We certainly had them all around, but I had never seen them attack anyone.

Well, in the heat we had a quick burial and that caused trouble. Actually it was Maggie who caused trouble by using the excuse of the quick burial to write to the authorities. She tried to get me involved but I kept out of it.

Chapter 4

A Trial, a Reappearance, and an Admirer

The upshot was Amanda Jane Spackford was put on trial for the murder of her husband, much to Maggie's delight. I refused to believe it and said as much. I went to the trial, as I wanted to tell everyone about the snake. I really should not have been there but I just could not keep away. As I sat there I saw someone that I knew. You could hardly miss him as he still bore the scar on his face that I had put there. I asked a soldier who was on duty there who the man with the scarred face was.

"Don't know his name. He's a convict. Employed in the central registry."

Someone else said that he was Jem Akenhead, transported for trying to steal plate from his employer. The soldier looked at me and smiled. I felt hot. Why was he smiling?

"What are you doing here miss?"

"I'm here because my mistress is charged with murder."

"Amanda Jane Spackford?"

"Yes."

He was called away but he smiled at me again as he left, and it was a friendly smile.

After some while the trial began and I heard both Maggie and Susan give evidence. Then my mistress went into the dock and it was then that I saw my friendly soldier behind her. Later on, at the adjournment, I came out for some air and came face to face with Jem. He stared at me until I said:

"Yes. It's really me."

He smiled, and it was not a friendly smile.

"Well, well," he said.

He was about to say something else when the soldier reappeared and came over to me.

"She's a plucky lass, your mistress."

He glanced at Jem.

"Something you want?"

"This dirty trollop caused this," he said, pointing to his scar.

"So?"

"I mean to have revenge. Damn my eyes if I don't"

He turned and was gone. I felt faint. I was helped to a bench in the shade. When I was recovered I found the soldier by me.

"Care to tell me what was that all about?"

I had never before told my side of the story and it gushed out of me now as if the soldier had plucked out a stopper. He listened carefully then said:

"Don't give it another thought. Leave all to me. Can you see me sometime?"

"Why?"

"So that I can reassure you that I have dealt with this."

And that was the first of many meetings. At the beginning he told me that he had arranged for Jem to be transferred a long way away. He explained that convicts who uttered threats could be moved, and he had spoken to the right person to get this done. Then, as I was not completely reassured, he offered to meet me again; and so it went on until one day he shocked me by kissing me! I drew back in a state of agitation asking him why he had done that. He told me that it was because he liked me and that it was not completely unknown for men who liked a young woman to steal a kiss.

"How can you like me?" I asked, touching my face.

"Because there is more to you than your face."

" I must go," I said.

I stood up. We had been sitting in Hyde Park.

"Before you go, say that you will see me again. Meet me here by the obelisk."

I nodded, and then fled.

Back in my little room I washed myself and changed into a nightgown. I then lay on my bed. It was too hot to sleep. In any case I wanted to think about what had happened to me. I had an admirer! I knew about this situation, having heard other young women talk about it as they cast pitying looks in my direction. Maggie Senchal had gone further and taunted me with the idea that I would never ever have someone interested in me. As I knew this to be true, her words did not bother me.

Just before I fell asleep it came to me. The thing that had been on my mind when James said obelisk. I remembered how it had been set up by the authorities and unveiled by the Mayor George Thornton. The joke was it is actually a sewer vent! The locals call it "Thornton's Scent Bottle".

But I am getting ahead of myself. My mistress was acquitted, as I was sure she would be. Both Maggie and Susan were sent packing as a consequence. Amanda Jane was able to use their lies to have her brought to court as a lever to dislodge them. The effect was wonderful. Up until then their presence had been poisonous, with Maggie using any and every situation to undermine Amanda Jane's authority, which had pretty well passed from Elias Spackford to Amanda.

I was sorry to see Sue go for it was clear as clear that she just used to do what Maggie told her. As she also did most of the laundry work, much of that came to me, another reason for me to regret losing her. In time we got more servants though, for England never seemed to tire of sending such young women out to us.

I still worried about them and Jem. Out of sight meant out of mind usually, but not for me. It was all very well for James to tell me that they would not bother us again, but bad pennies have a habit of turning up. James O'Brian, my soldier, intended to serve out his time in the army and try his luck in Sydney. Would I wait for him? Would I?

Chapter 5

Two Marriages

Our household ran along smoothly. With more servants taken on, I was given more responsibility, as Amanda Jane was busy trying to improve her stock. So it often fell to me to organise the dinners that we had with various gentlemen in attendance, including Arthur Spens, the lawyer who defended Amanda. To be honest I thought he was spineless. I know that sounds harsh, but his defence wasn't all that good. It was only when the court accepted the notes of the doctor who came when Mr Spackford died that she got off. I reckon that I could have done as good a job. He mooned about too, worried about his wife when he should have been getting on with things. Still, Amanda seemed to like him.

She was trying to find out what had happened to her parents at this time and Arthur Spens was helping her. But, just as you would imagine, he proved as useless in this endeavour as any other. He introduced Amanda to the Saverys expecting them to help her. They proved to be useless. Savery really was a gentleman; a forger who was nearly hanged for his efforts, and only just avoided that extreme penalty by being transported. He had a silver tongue and had won many people over since his arrival in New South Wales. He managed to persuade many that he was keen to rehabilitate himself and gain respectability. Somehow, I suppose by flattery and so on, he had been able to get into the Colonial Secretary's office.

He then petitioned for his wife to join him, with some success, I might add, for the next we all heard was that Mrs Savery had arrived. She came in circumstances that were considered to be far from respectable, because she had become extremely close friends on board her ship with a Mr Algernon Montagu, who was on his way to Tasmania to become Attorney General. Everyone then heard that the Saverys, as a result, had had an almost fatal quarrel, because at the end of it, Savery had cut his throat in a bid to commit suicide. He had been saved by a doctor who had been called immediately.

It was all in the papers, which seized upon this scandal, as they did any such thing, in order to sell more copies. Arthur Spens, poor fool, tried to keep himself above such matters, so he did not read about it. Would you believe it, he tried to tell Amanda Jane that it was confidential! I know for a fact that Savery tried to get his wife to find out about Amanda Jane's Ma and Pa, and Amanda Jane went to see her, but got no news from that quarter.

I felt for her, I really did, as she tried to establish whether her Ma and Pa were still in this world. I had set my face against any such action myself having decided long since that the present was important. The past was just that, the past. We live in the present with any hopes we might have set in the future. My dreams were now fixed on a future with James O'Brian. I tried to hold myself in check telling no one about him and my dreams, not even Amanda. She now had to cope with Arthur Spens, for his wife had died and he took it hard. As I said, he was a pretty poor specimen, getting all soft because of a death. It wasn't a love match in the first case, but one founded upon a generous dowry and the continued support of her family, so I heard tell.

Everything ran reasonably well for some time until one day when an officer called and left a note for Mrs Amanda Jane Spackford. That night I saw her leave the house and later return. She went unaccompanied, and for the following few days she was very agitated. I thought that it was Arthur Spens' proposal of marriage that was troubling her. I learned about this a few days later. In the meantime I met James and he said that as he had been of some assistance to my employer she had agreed for my release to be married. I pressed him to tell in what fashion he had been able to assist her, but he refused to tell me, saying that all would be revealed in good time. I supposed that this was all to do with Maggie and Jem so I held my peace.

A few days later Arthur Spens was with Amanda and as I knew something was in the wind I stayed nearby. Eventually I couldn't stand it any longer, so I went in to ask if they required anything. Amanda and Arthur looked sheepish at first, then, Amanda said that I was to bring in some champagne and glasses, enough for everyone, as they had to tell us all something. I ran back to the kitchen and told all the others. Cook said immediately that he had proposed to her. I knew that she was right. I went back with the bottles (I took two) and glasses and everyone crowded in after me. Arthur made a great fuss of opening the bottles, one of which ran over onto the drugget. I mopped it up with a cloth. He filled the glasses and sat down.

There was a pause, and after Amanda said, "Well go on" quietly, Arthur said, really nervously:

" I would like you all to drink the health of the future Mr and Mrs Arthur Spens, as Amanda Jane has done me the great honour agreeing to be my wife".

Everyone drank and Cook cried, wiping her eyes with her big red hands. We all clapped our hands as if we were in a theatre. Amanda asked us not to applaud her which made us all do it again as Arthur, at last! kissed her. Emboldened by the wine   and the knowledge that James had spoken to Amanda I went to the centre of the room. I think everyone, except perhaps Amanda, thought that I was going to say something on behalf of all the staff. Instead I said:

"I also have an announcement. Mr James O'Brian, who soon will be a soldier no more, and I are to be wed too."

There was a gasp and then a hush. I hurried to fill it with:

"Please wish us well."

I cannot remember much after that. I took a big gulp of the fizzy wine to cover the pause. I think someone said:

"Good luck to you and your soldier!"

I do remember though that Amanda embraced me and said that she and Arthur would be giving us a dowry. I began to collect the empty glasses as Arthur and Amanda whispered together. She said forcefully:

"Yes, yes, you must, you really must."

Arthur, looking furious, then told me that it would give him great pleasure if I were to allow him to give me away.

Arthur and Amada's wedding was a grand affair with more champagne and a truly magnificent cake produced by Cook. I married James O'Brian in a much smaller ceremony where, true to his word, I was given away by Arthur Spens. We celebrated with a dance where many of James' regimental friends came, and I'm sorry to say, many got very drunk. They were mainly simple soldiers, but he also had a few civilians, traders and suchlike, including one or two who had shops. Later that night Jamie was kind and considerate, but insistent, and so I entered the state of marriage, and almost immediately did what it says in the marriage service: I began to beget children.

Chapter 6

A Mysterious Death of an Officer

We had a few days together in what passed as a hotel. A few days later, in the morning, as he was shaving, something that intrigued me, never having seen this operation before, he said that he had something to tell me. It concerns Amanda Jane, he told me. We sat at breakfast and he told me the following story.

"Your Amanda Jane was abandoned in England by a certain Captain Frederick Paffrey who pretended to marry her. Because of his actions she eventually stole something and was transported. He came to New South Wales recently, and I knew him because we served together in the Fifty-Third Regiment in that abortive sweep in Tasmania. One night in Tasmania when he was in charge of the guard, and had had too much to drink, he boasted to me that he had not only managed to rid himself of a pretty but inconvenient wife abroad, but had also ill-used several young women in the past in England, and that one in particular had finished up as a convict. He told me that he had not only turned her head and persuaded her to run away with him, but had also stolen her father's watch, presuming that the father would assume that his daughter had stolen it to maintain herself. Later, no doubt when he became sober, he realised that he had confessed to someone who was now a danger to him. As it was dark he did not know who the soldier was.

But when the officer examined the muster records as part of his regimental duties I was not shown to be on duty that night. A Private, Percival Flight was marked down as being on picket duty that night instead. It was this soldier that I stood in for because Percival had a bout of the flux.

Maybe you have heard that some soldiers were shot by accident and died during this shocking affair?"

I said that I had heard about this.

"Well, later the following day, following some confusion by an apparently erroneous sighting of a native, Private Flight was shot, apparently in error. Of course the officer was exonerated, it was a terrible mistake, but mistakes do happen. When we returned to Sydney I determined to keep a close eye on this officer, and, if I got the chance I would get revenge for poor Percival. So I was in Hyde Park when he met Amanda Jane. He blackmailed her and when he went I spoke to her. I told her that I recognised her as I had been on duty in the court when she was tried. I told her to go home and say nothing."

James then produced a copy of the newspaper, where I read:

MYSTERIOUS DEATH OF OFFICER

On Wednesday night the body of Captain Paffrey of the 53rd (Shropshire) Regiment of Foot was discovered near one of the large trees that remain in Hyde Park. His throat had been cut and nothing remained in his pockets thus giving credence to the theory that he had been the victim of a foul robbery.

His body had apparently lain there most of the night. A half smoked cheroot lay nearby. The brand was a popular one with military gentlemen.

Captain Paffrey had recently taken part in the largely abortive sweep in Tasmania where his conduct as an officer gave cause for concern. An undisclosed source of information indicated that he was not the most popular of officers, and having completed some time in Australia, where he was attached to the 53rd Regiment, was due to return to England.

We can reveal that he had made enquiries about travelling on the Sarah, but had not finalised his arrangements.

We have repeatedly warned the Governor General that the city is still a dangerous place. Since the Hyde Park Barracks were built more ruffians have been placed in them and we urge the authorities to maintain their vigilance in respect of containing them to the safety of the public.

My hands flew to my throat. Was I married to a murderer? James, seeing my expression and alarm, laughed.

"I was in the park ready to do whatever was necessary to protect Amanda. I was going to confront him, hoping that as I knew so much about him I could persuade him to leave her alone, but I was too late. I heard a cry and saw his cheroot fall out of his mouth as he fell. Then I saw, crouching over him, a black man taking things from his pockets. The blood was everywhere having come from a gash in his throat, but he was dead for his main artery had been severed. The blackfella did not try to run away. I asked why he had killed a white man and he said that this was a bad man who he had to kill for the sake of his tribe. I picked up a watch and asked if he wanted it. He said that I might have it. He said to me that it was useless as you couldn't eat it or use it in any way. So I asked what he was going to do with the white man's things and he told me that they must be destroyed for they were tabu. He wrapped them up in some cloth made from some sort of bark and disappeared with them into the hot night. "

James cut out the item from the newspaper and wrote upon it:

Do nothing.   Tell no one.

He then told me to take it to Amanda Jane and tell her that it was all over now. I did as I was bid. I went straight to her, and shutting ourselves in the reception room, I showed her the newspaper. Once she had read it I screwed up the paper

36

making it into a spill to light a candle and dropped it into the grate. When she tried to speak I shook my head and told her to go down to the ship that had brought in the stock that she had ordered. I thought it best to divert her from thinking about what could not be changed now.

I didn't go with her to the harbour, so I didn't meet Abel Magwitch, the man who was to have such an impact on her life and on mine. Nor did I meet the ship's carpenter, Alfred Trimble, who had done some work on one occasion for her husband. Once she had brought her precious rams back to the farm she told me how, as she had collected them, Abel had recognised her.

"Just think, after all these years", she said, not able to resist a look in a mirror.

" He was a shepherd who directed me to a farrier. I was running away to meet my sweetheart when my mare cast a shoe."

So, now I heard from her how she had run off to Portsmouth where her beau had 'married' her, then abandoned her when his regiment sailed for India. It was the story that James had told me, but I listened patiently.

The next we heard of Abel was that he had gone to work at Vaucluse, helping the carpenter, who somehow owed him a favour. From there, he was plucked from assisting the carpenter by a farmer who needed someone who was clever with sheep. Into the vast interior he went and we heard nothing more from him until, after some years, he came to ask Amanda Jane for some help.

Chapter 7

Bookselling

Although my husband could have had a grant of land, had he so wished, he rejected the idea, saying that he was a town boy and no clodhopping farmer. He had taken my dowry gratefully and we set up a small shop with it, where he told me the secret of success was not to sell people what they needed, but to sell them what the shopkeeper persuaded them they wanted. And what people wanted, he was going to persuade them was books.

I was doubtful. Could we really make a living from selling books? I was persuaded when Jamie showed me a case full of them that he had bought at the docks. "They were brought in by a fellow with the same idea as me", he told me. "But as we already have a shop we can steal a march on him. In any case by the time that he sets up there will be demand enough for more than one shop." Jamie was right. In two days we had sold all the books so we sought out Alfred Trimble and asked him to bring us more.

What we had sold more than covered our outgoings until we had more stock. And we also sold papers and inks to a continuing group of regular customers. In time we worked out how to get a steady supply of books and I was pleased to say that we developed such a good reputation that our name was good in London for many an order. Many of the books made no sense to me, but they sold. Some, the novels, I enjoyed. My book learning was paying off too, for I was able to talk with some knowledge about the books as we sold them. It's always a good idea to know what it is you are selling.

In time we had two children, both bonny, and to my delight, not one inheriting my looks. Young Jamie took after his dad but was a mite more thoughtful. Olivia could be a dreamy lass, maybe because of the books that she was able to stick her nose into at any time of day or night. She really took after me! We had a shop assistant, a young man, Toby Davis, who was the son of a Government man, though you would scarce credit it to look at him. He was really Tobias, but was always called Toby. Although he was on the short side, a more industrious and trustworthy fellow you would have to walk many miles to find. We also had a very attractive maid, Lizbeth Wright, another offspring of a convict, but I had to close my eyes and ears as to who her mother was. In all my life I never once called her Elizabeth, her real Christian name, nor to my knowledge did any one else.

At first I was doubtful about employing her for I could close my ears but once you have heard something it stays with you. Then I thought what a shame it was not to give someone their chance. I had been given mine when I was chosen at Parramatta that time. To be honest I considered that with her parentage she could be employed to do the rough work; if she didn't like that I could send her packing with a clear conscience.

She had a sunny disposition, worked hard, never complained and soon enough I could not imagine our household without her. I would sit in our back room, with my stays loosened, listening to her singing as she dealt with whatever had to be done. Because she was so quick I had my work cut out to keep her busy all the time, which I needed to do, as she was too ready to dally in the front of the shop, smiling at young men customers when she had finished her tasks. Then I caught on. When she was around we had many more young men seeking a suitable book to give to an aunt or uncle, so I did more of her work myself and put her to the selling side.

When she had agreed a sale, Toby would step in to complete it. Jamie had his doubts about the morality of such a way to get customers, so I reminded him how the serving girls in the places where he took the occasional drink with his old army friends were usually the prettiest girls. Toby was not that clever at dealing with the customers. Well, he hardly had the looks nor the charm of Lizbeth. The men customers preferred her. He was adequate when it came to dealing with women, who liked the patient way he had with them all, but he was clearly fond of my Olivia. Later on, when my Jamie died, Toby was steadfast in my support. I am sure that he did not know about Badger's plan. As Olivia grew up he became even fonder of her, as anyone could tell by the way he looked at her. She, by contrast, grew less so. I noticed that, after her Pa died, she changed somewhat, became colder, more distant. Not to me, nor Lizbeth, but to most men in general, and Toby, in particular.

All would have gone well had I not spied a face one day that I did not wish ever to see in all my life. It was Jem Akenhead, looking quite prosperous. He seemed to have done well for himself, judging by his clothes that were certainly as good as any that my Jamie wore. He still had that mark on his face, which was brown from the sun. I saw him looking in the window of our shop and though I tried to slip out to the back he saw me and came in. I stood still and waited. He did not keep me waiting long. Dismissing Toby with a wave of his hand he leaned close to me and claimed that he was interested in buying something about arson.

"It's an interest that I have. It's surprising how many shops for example catch fire. Mind you there are many ways to prevent a fire."

He smiled that nasty smile that I remembered and left us. I told Jamie when he came in and he looked extremely troubled.

"He's got in with a bad group. I thought that we had seen the last of him, but it seems that he has a line in blackmail going on. They never actually threaten anyone but the hints that they drop lets you know what they can do if you ignore them."

"But can't you speak to anyone like you did before?"

"Not any more. I'm just an old soldier now. It was different when I had the ear of people who I could do a favour. I can't do much now."

Chapter 8

Arson

The first attempt was not very successful; as it was not intended to do much damage, just act as a warning. Some pieces of paper were left burning in the yard. We ignored it and were told by our friends in a neighbouring shop that we were stupid not to pay. The next time I caught it just in time to prevent real damage so we knew that they were in earnest. I tried to get Arthur Spens interested but he was unwilling to be drawn into something where he said there was little proof on our part. I had always been wary of that man. He was far too ready to give in. I remembered him at the trial when Amanda Jane was brought up for murder. He was pretty ineffectual then. I took the precaution of making sure that Jamie and Olivia were lodging elsewhere, and for a while nothing more happened.

The smell of burning paper woke me. The blast of heat that came at me as I came downstairs singed my hair. Behind me Jamie coughed and fell down pushing me forward so that I hit my head on the banister. Toby pulled at my arms to make me stand up, then he pushed me aside to grab Jamie who was still on the floor.

"Get out! Get out! " He shouted.

"No, not without James."

Together we dragged him across the floor and through the front door where others took over the task of getting him clear. I turned to go back.

"No! For God's sake. Stay here."

Hands seized me, preventing me from returning, pushing me down. I was crying. It was emotion, fear and anger as well as the smoke.

"Lizbeth"

"She's out already."

I relaxed, and as I did so, they let go of me. Pushing myself up, I ran back in round to the back of the counter and, opening the cupboard, I pulled out the bundle that I had previously placed there. Holding it against my chest I ran back. Then I started to cry and shake still holding on to the bundle, which I would not let go of until I came to little Jamie and Olivia. Handing over the bundle, I held them fiercely until Jamie said:

"You're hurting me Mama."

Going through our poor shop's mess the following day was a sorry business. We lost all our stock that was in the shop that night. I was right to insist that the children were not above the shop. Luckily we were between deliveries so, as I turned over burned and wet books and paper, I calculated that we had not lost too much in cash terms. Jamie was furious. I think that he imagined that if we had stood up to Jem he would have gone off to try to terrorise others instead. I had another opinion. Jem was so well dressed that it made me think that he had others behind him.

"He's nothing. A puffed up nothing who thinks that he can menace us all and we'll simply collapse."

"I'm not so sure Jamie. I think Jem is only part of something. He's a front man, but I'm sure that not only does he merely insinuate, but he also avoids actually dirtying his hands. Is there any way that we can find out who might be behind him?"

Jamie poked with his toe at a sodden mass of papers that had been a copy of 'Bleak House'.

"I will give it some thought. Badger might have some ideas."

I did not like the idea of involving Badger Brill, an old companion of my husband. I suspected that any ideas that he might have would involve some form of brutality, as usual. As a soldier he had been lashed fairly often and declared that it never did him any harm.

Jamie, seeing my expression, laughed, and said:

"Don't worry. I'll only talk to Badge. Meantime I must see about getting another shop. There might be one in Erskine or Margaret Street. It's lucky that we were only renting this one. He stood up, still straight and tall as ever he had been when a soldier and marched off, feet crunching broken glass and wet cinders. I watched him walk away, his stride and bearing proclaiming his past to those who could read it. I called to Toby and to Lizbeth to help me clear up, and we set to, throwing out the wet smelly mess into the yard. I knew that I could rely upon Jamie to get on with things; a true man of action, he would have us in business in a trice, but I was still worried about Badger being involved. And, it turned out that I was right to be concerned.

Chapter 9

A Plan

Listeners never hear anything good about themselves, and I had often warned my children not to listen outside doors, but when Badge came back with my husband and settled themselves in our newly rented shop I was overcome with curiosity. 'Curiosity killed the cat' was what my mother used to say to me. She also reckoned that 'Little pitchers have long ears'. When I worked for Amanda Jane I often listened at doors. It's something that all servants do as a matter of course. It usually means that they know just about everything that's going on in any household where they are employed, and it can work to the advantage of the master and mistress. Having said that, I must admit that a servant's life is generally so limited and dull that knowing all that goes on gives some spice to an otherwise dull existence. It also means that whoever hears anything has the pleasure of passing on their intelligence to others.

I hoped to hear what they planned to do about Jem and I was not disappointed. Their plan was to discredit him in some way with the authorities so that he was taken up and appeared before a magistrate. If they were successful Jem might be removed to work out somewhere far away. How to do this was the problem. I listened to them and could not resist joining them. Setting before them some bacon, liver and onions, a favourite of Mr Brill, and a bottle of gin, a favourite of both of them, I sat down.

"Thank you very kindly for the grub and the booze, but we don't need you now", said Badger in his usual forthright way.

I noticed that he was still a stranger to soap and water, but I tried not to breathe too deeply near him. Badger made up for the lack of hair upon his head with a mighty surplus on the rest of his body some of which poked out from the top of his shirt. Not tall, his head seemed to fit onto his body without the benefit of a neck, and his face, even in repose was undeniably ugly. When he smiled people recoiled for his teeth were more repellent than his visage. I never ever saw him in other than boots, whatever the weather. Jamie told me it was on account of snakes. Jamie told me that he was mortal affeared of them; it was the one thing that he was affeared of.

I waited until he and Jamie were punishing the food, and some of the gin had gone in on top of it.

"Oh! But you do need me."

"And why pray is that?"

"Because I know master Jem Akenhead and his weaknesses."

"Which are?"

"Young naive women and pride in his appearance. He is a vain lecher. Bait your trap with both and you may catch him."

"What do you suggest?"

"Put a suitable young woman into his path who tells him that she can find her way to allow him to get at her master's money. Make sure that she seems young and foolish and apparently overcome with his manliness and dashing appearance. He will find it difficult to resist her. Despite all, he is as stupid as most men, when they think some female is interested in them."

Jamie and Badge looked at each other.

I held my breath for a moment. Had I gone too far? Men like to think that they are the clever ones.   With more time I would have tried to be more, what was that word that Amanda used to use, subtle, but I did not have more time. I tried to look indifferent.

"You are quite right my dear", said Badger.

"We had in fact worked out such a scheme ourselves."

He looked meaningfully at Jamie who seemed bemused.

"The only problem is where do we get such a young woman who fits the bill and would be amenable to acting as we suggest?"

I said nothing but looked equally meaningfully at the front of the shop.   Both men followed my gaze and saw Lizbeth. We all stood up and moved towards the front of the shop where Lizbeth was serving a young man.

" It's exactly the sort of book that a respectable lady would wish to receive from her nephew. We sell many such, and have never had any complaints."

49

"Lizbeth, my dear, can you leave this gentleman to be served by Toby", I said motioning with my hand to bring Toby forward.

The 'gentleman', as big a ruffian as ever I did see, looked disappointed, dropped the book that he was holding upside down, and stalked out of the shop. Lizbeth looked alarmed. She took the kerchief from round her neck and wiped her face. I told her that nothing was wrong. We merely wished to ask her a few questions. Seated all together in the back room and ignoring the smell of fried liver and onions that still hung in the air, I asked Lizbeth if she knew Jem. She looked puzzled. I added that he had been to the shop on several occasions, that his full name was Jem Akenhead. I then described him. My description of a slim, smartly dressed man, a bit of a fop, with a scar on his face, drew no look of recognition from Lizbeth.

"No, no, I can't remember any one like that".

Her answer brought sighs of satisfaction from Jamie and Badger.

"You're sure now, absolutely sure."

"I'm totally sure. I would remember someone with a scarred disfigured face wouldn't I?"

As she said this she caught my eye and went red. I ignored her blushes. I was used to ignoring all sorts of reactions to my own poor face.

"How much does Mr O'Brian pay you", began Badger.

"Mr Brill means would you like to earn a guinea?" I cut in.

The pinkness went from her face to be replaced with a look of greed, then, just as quickly, a look of suspicion.

"What do I have to do? I'm a decent girl."

"We are all aware of that. That's why we employ you here in a decent respectable establishment. We need your help. We want to play a trick upon Jem Akenhead. That's why it is important that he should not have seen you before. You are sure that he has not set eyes on you at some time?"

"How can I be sure of that? Lots of men look at me. Lots that I see. Probably lots that I don't see."

This last remark was delivered with some satisfaction.

"Just so, Just so. What we require of you,"I began.

Both Badger and Jamie stood up. Jamie said that in the circumstances it might be best if he and Lizbeth and Badge went to a quieter place to explain what they had in mind. His wink to me told me that I was to agree, so I nodded and said that with only Toby in the shop it might be best if I were to join him so as not to lose customers, nor stock to thieves, Sydney still having plenty of these.

Chapter 10

The Plan Goes Wrong

In essence it was to be a sort of buttock and twang, and I was doubtful that Jem would be taken in by such an old device. At least Lizbeth listened carefully to her instructions. Both Jamie and Badge were at pains to reassure her that at no time would they not be nearby. She would not see them, but they would be there. It would be Badger who would spring the trap once Lizbeth had snared Jem. It was essential that Jem did not see Jamie. Over and over they emphasised this until I told them to stop, as they were making her nervous.

Several days went by before Jem put in an appearance. His entering our shop made my stomach feel queer. I can't think of anyone that I hated so much that it made me feel faint to be civil to him. I knew from the others how much would buy him off so I had it ready in a packet. He sneered at me as he took it.

"You think you are so high and mighty. You think that because you are running a respectable business that someone like me can't touch you."

I said nothing. He pocketed the money and sauntered out smiling. I knew that he would now be shadowed and sure enough he was by Badger whose abilities in this art had been honed to a high state of perfection. It was Badger who told me later what subsequently happened. I made him tell me the whole story even though it sickened me to hear the details. I forced myself to listen to punish myself for being a party to such a stupid endeavour.

Followed by Badger, he went straight to a drinking den where he immediately began to run through what I had given him. Badger sent for Lizbeth who had been kept quietly out of sight at home feigning illness. She now came into the game playing the part of a simple quietly dressed maid. Sitting in the corner she was ignored by Jem at first who still drank and treated others as if he was never ever going to be short of money. Eventually he drifted over to Lizbeth who played her part by smiling shyly and laughing at his witticisms. She explained that she was supposed to meet her Pa in the bar to collect some money from him as soon as he was paid and before he spent it all on rum.

After a while she said that she must have missed him, or perhaps he had gone to another bar. She rose, put on her bonnet and started to leave. Jem played the gentleman and offered to escort her home. She feigned doubtfulness, which only inflamed Jem more. At last she agreed reluctantly that he might escort her. Her instructions were to make sure that she chose a dark alley and to be ready to run off as soon as Badger appeared. There was no shortage of back alleyways so she quickly turned down one. Badger duly caught up with them and accused Jem of trying to seduce his daughter. Instead of running away immediately Lizbeth left it too late and Jem seized her, drawing her to him as protection. No stranger to what went on in Sydney each night, he surmised quite correctly that he was in line to be a victim of some sort of attack. He drew a knife and holding it to Lizbeth's neck he forced her onto her knees. Apparently his intention was to make Badger back off sufficiently so that he could run off.

Unknown To Jem however, Jamie had quietly come up the alley from the other direction. He jumped upon Jem who, in spinning round, caught Jamie a blow in his belly with his knife. Jamie staggered to his knees. Jem brought his leg up smartly under Jamie's chin , and then dropping a now petrified Lizbeth, ran away. By the time that Badger got to Jamie he had already lost a lot of blood. Badger pushed his kerchief into the wound and managed to staunch it. Lizbeth had now, at last, run off, so Badger took Jamie back to the drinking den. There they were refused entry because the owner feared the traps, so Badger took Jamie on his back and brought him home to me. Both of them, covered in blood, came in the side way and Badger, by now nearly all in, dropped Jamie into a chair where he sat motionless. Despite all I could do he died that night.

When I told Amanda Jane that my Jamie was dead I handed over the watch that he had given me as I thought that it was time that she had it along with the story of how it had come into my possession. When she asked what I would do now I said that I would continue with the shop. We were doing quite well now, and in addition to the books we were also selling bookshelves. My plan was to get my young son Jamie apprenticed to a carpenter, as he seemed to have some skill in that direction. Olivia could help in the shop until she was wed. Sometimes she drove me to distraction with her dreamy ways, always with her nose in a book, but what else could I expect with her living over a bookshop? I also hoped that I might get some sympathy and assistance over my problems with Jem Akenhead. I thought that as he had run off, not having been caught and taken before a Magistrate, for an attempted rape of our servant girl, he was likely to make more mischief for me. Then my nerve failed me. If I asked for help I would have to confess how we had planned to trap Jem. So I left Amanda Jane and came back to my shop.

There I found Badger who had obviously been drinking. He bad me send the children away and when I had seen them safely with a neighbour he said:

"You know what we must do now, don't you?"

I shook my head. I had no idea how to proceed.

"We must do what your husband did with that captain."

"But he was attacked by a black native. Jamie saw him. He told me all about it. I have just come from taking the watch that he retrieved back to its rightful owner."

Badger laughed.

"So that's what he told you. I wondered why you hadn't been upset. He didn't tell you that he and me arranged it all?"

I felt faint. I sat on a chair and Badger said anxiously:

"Now then, hold up. Don't go all soft of a sudden. You're made of sterner stuff, I know!"

Badger poured me a dram. I drank it shakily, spilling some. I wiped it off me mechanically. The smell of rum made me feel sick. Strangely it brought back memories of my time in the boat when I had been transported. I had survived worse then, I told myself. I can survive this. Badger eyed me cautiously.

"I wondered what Jamie told you. He said that when he married you he confessed about the captain as he didn't want you to find out from someone else."

"But the native, the tribesman, the blackfella......"

"Jamie could always produce a good tale. How else do you survive in the army? How do you think he survived? Oh! I don't mean that he was an out and out liar, but he could add sufficient details to a story to make it that bit more acceptable."

" I thought I knew the truth."

"Now truth is something that is always in short supply. Tell me, what do you say to your customers when you are behindhand with their order for a bookcase? Well?

I bowed my head. He was right, of course. But what I called little white lies were surely in a different class. I had to use the occasional tarradiddle to help my business. Without such an action my children would not have a roof over their heads nor bread in their mouths. As I thought it, I knew that if I spoke it, it would seem a thin excuse. I shook my head, not in negation but to clear it.

"So, what can we do?"

Badger poured himself another helping of rum. He smiled. He said:

"Leave it all to me. I'll do what I wanted to do in the first case. I'll do it my way, the way I suggested but what Jamie said no to. He had gone soft. If we had acted swiftly and firmly this would all have been over now and he would be here with us taking a glass in celebration. And it will not only finish this but it will also send a message to any others who might have similar ideas about taking your money."

Chapter 11

A solution

Looking back on all this I realise that I could have gone to the authorities. Such an idea would have horrified Badger whose experience of life had taught him how to preserve himself and his mates. So I simply left him to deal with it, as he wanted. A body was pulled out of Neutral Bay a few days later.

Going to the authorities would have meant drawing attention to myself, something that I desperately wished to avoid. Sydney might have become more civilised and tolerant but it still had its share of young girls who needed my help. I knew what I did was not accepted by many, particularly the churches and churchmen. My activities were also denounced by many God fearing women. I also knew that some doctors with richer patients than I dealt with, did what I did, but concealed their activities within the medical establishment with medical terms that put them beyond the law. What I did was illegal.

The story that appeared in the local newspaper was that a government man had been visiting a foreign ship that was anchored in Neutral bay. It was unclear why he had gone there, some said that he had been invited by a Dutch crew member; others said that he had been drinking in a tavern and had been taken on board dead drunk; yet another story involved a young woman whose morals were questionable. Whatever the beginnings, the end was that he finished up in the sea being washed to and fro with the rubbish that was thrown overboard by the ships in the harbour. By the time that he was dragged out he had been badly mauled by sharks, but enough remained of him for him to be identified as Jem Akenhead. No one came forward to claim the body so he was quickly interred.

For some while I worried that his mates might take up where he had left off, seeking not only to batten upon a poor widow woman, but also to revenge his death. I slept each night with a carving knife beside me ready to defend myself and my two children. I never had to use it, for which I give thanks.

Chapter 12

Magwitch inherits

It was about this time that Abel Magwitch's employer died. Abel came looking for some help and naturally sought out Amanda Jane. Like many a person before me, and, I suppose, many more in the future, I eavesdropped and heard him tell her what had happened. I was visiting and chatting with Cook when he arrived, so I moved quietly into a side room and sat out of sight, as I wanted to know why he had come to see her.

They were out in the wilds looking for stray sheep. Then some local natives approached them, all covered with white clay. They carried those spears that the blackies have, nasty ugly weapons, and Abel knew that something was wrong. He told the others to get away. But before they could do so one of the blackies speared one of the men. They also speared Abel's master, but before he fell down he drew a pistol and shot one of the natives. He gave his other gun to Abel telling him to shoot. Abel did so hitting another blackie and the natives ran off.

Abel carried his master back on his master's horse, as he could not ride. Then, although he got him back safely, he died.

Before he died, he told Abel that he had made him his heir, having no living relatives. He died that night as Abel sat with him. Abel showed Amanda Jane a will. I saw it too as I took in some tea for them both. So Abel was quite the hero!

Well, Amanda Jane looked at the will, and using her husband, who was a lawyer; she determined that it was in order. I later found out that Arthur had advised her to help Abel, as the homestead that Abel had inherited was quite large and valuable, and it could be to her benefit in the future. That was typical of that man, always making sure that he got something from everything that he touched. So she advanced monies to Abel Magwitch who built up the spread to be even more valuable. During all this time Alfred Trimble was still coming to New South Wales, and because I used him to bring me fresh stock I got to know the story of how he took money back with him from Abel to give to a lawyer called Jaggers. The money was to fund the making of a gentleman. I snorted when I first heard about it. As if money could change a blacksmith to a real gentleman!

Poor Abel was totally set on this lad of his, particularly when Alfred brought him news as to how his protégé was progressing. As you might imagine, he was running through Abel's money like a Lord. This didn't worry Abel, as he seemed to think that the lad would scarcely be a gentleman, were he not to throw other folks hard-earned cash around.

The trouble was, Abel then got it into his head that he must go to see the boy! Naturally everyone tried to dissuade him, but all to no avail. In the end they gave in and hatched a plan.

Although I was not supposed to know about the plan to get Magwitch to England, Amanda Jane could scarcely hide it from me. In the end she took me wholly into her confidence. I thought she was mad. I thought they all were. To risk all for a boy in England that Magwitch hadn't seen in years!

She explained that they were all to go on board a ship in Sydney Harbour for a meal. After dinner, a man dressed as Magwitch, would leave the ship. While he did so Abel would retire to a cabin where the captain, who would not be in the plot, would know him as Mr Provis. I suggested that the man dressed as Abel should pretend to be ill at first. He should then ride out well beyond Bathurst avoiding everyone. As my mother was wont to say: 'Out of sight, out of mind'. His people would put it out that he had gone round his spread on a tour of inspection. By the time he had come back Mr Provis would be well on his way. The second part of the plan was that Abel, once he had seen Pip, would come back to New South Wales, still as Mr Provis. A lot depended on no one wanting to see Abel Magwitch in all the time that he was abroad. Given how remote the spread that Abel had inherited was, it might just work.

I had to agree that as Amanda Jane had helped Abel once before when he had come to her for assistance, she ought to continue to help him now. I begged her not to let Arthur know anything about this conspiracy. She had told Abel that Arthur was involved, but this was not true. It seemed however that this lie made Abel do what was necessary to keep him safe. Actually it was not difficult to leave Arthur out, for he was such a self-centred man who was so concerned with his own affairs, that he was uninterested in his wife's activities in general. Over the years I had determined that he was a feeble specimen of manhood who used others shamelessly. He thought he was so clever being a lawyer, but there were many, including his wife, who could run rings about him. I did not worry about him, but about the fact that he was just as likely to tell all to some of his high and mighty chums. I remember how they used to talk over dinners that Amanda Jane and I got ready for them in the old days. Once they had got a skin-full, there was no knowing what they would say. The things that I could tell you about some folk in New South Wales!

I could also tell a few tales to do with what I also did some days when called upon. It started when I had children and got to know a woman who "assisted" me when I was in the last stages of my labour. She was scarcely a midwife, but knew about such matters so came out if asked. It was her accounts of poor girls who had got into trouble that intrigued me. Without actually saying how she did it, she let on that she "helped" them. Then one night she came to see me in a terrible fix. Her normal helper had died. She just wanted someone to give a hand. I would not have to do anything, just be there and maybe comfort the girl. I was hooked. From then on I turned out to help in all sorts of weathers and when my mentor died it seemed a natural thing to take up the burden. We had a way that you could ask for help. You came to the shop and asked for a particular book. Naturally I told no one, not even Amanda Jane about this part of my life.

When Amanda Jane told me that he was to be knighted I had to stop myself from laughing, as she seemed to think it was important. Then, as we sat and had a drink together, she said that, although she would soon be Lady Spens, all she could really think about when Arthur told her, was Arthur in his drawers walking about the bedroom, bleating on about not being able to find his shirts. We laughed. Men!

"So I suppose you will have nothing to do with your old acquaintances, now you are to be a real lady."

"Do not, I beg you, believe that of me. Have we not been so close that on occasions we have been almost like sisters?"

I looked at her steadily. She blushed, and it wasn't the wine. She knew that, close as we might have been, there was a gulf between us, fixed by the life that she led at a level that I would never reach. She was just naturally my superior. That's how life is. Now, I know some would say 'sour grapes' but I truly didn't mind. I was married and had my children; something that I had never ever considered would happen to me, poor 'Plain Jane'.

Chapter 13

Olivia and Jamie

Living in bookshops has considerable compensations if you enjoy reading. I did. When trade was slow I read. So did Olivia who both pleased and exasperated me, as she was able to read and write so much earlier in life than I ever could. She was a loving and kind child and I tried not to favour her over her brother, treating both she and Jamie the same in every respect. I was deluding myself. It's very hard to treat two children exactly the same, especially when they are brother and sister, and have different gifts and temperaments. James was different. It was obvious that Jamie was his favourite, but that never seemed to bother Livvy. I considered that fact to be inevitable in the male dominated society that existed in and around Sydney, and so, apparently, did she.

I often embraced both Olivia and Jamie, giving them the love that I had missed in my early years. In time my kisses were lost on Jamie, as he grew older and wriggled free from my clasp when I clutched him. Olivia continued to enjoy my manifestations of love. She told me later in her life, when she had grown up, that she felt that she was being drawn into a feminine world with female secrets that would be forbidden to boys and men. She regarded Lizbeth as part of that feminine conspiracy which manifested itself in murmured conversations that were broken off when Pa or Jamie or Toby came near. She never commented on Lizbeth's dark complexion. I suppose as no one else said anything, neither did she.

Jamie was indulged by his pa, but was still sent to school where he suffered in having his head stuffed with Latin, Greek, natural sciences and other useless learning. Jamie said that if his son was to make anything of his life he had to be educated. He ignored his son's cleverness with his hands. On one occasion Jamie said that he hated school and all the book learning; he wanted to be a soldier as his Pa had been once. He made the mistake of saying this to James, and this provoked such an angry outburst that Olivia fled under the table clearly frightened of her father. I worried about Jamie when he came home from school almost in tears. He was so young and seemed so vulnerable. His Pa said that even if he was not to be a soldier he still needed to know how to stand up for himself.

When my husband died Jamie seemed to change over night. Someone, it might have been Amanda Jane, said to him that he was the man of the house now, and he seemed to take this seriously. From that time on he settled at school, and when he finished he told me that he wanted to be a carpenter like Alfred Trimble. Arthur helped me get him a place with a joiner, saying that as Jamie was already quite skilled he should follow that trade.

Olivia never seemed jealous of her brother, despite the fact that her schooling was accomplished at home. She did not go to a scholastic establishment like Jamie. She said that she had her books, and they were her academy. Through them she visited other lands, and explored deserts, jungles and every other sort of parts of the world that had been written about.

James and I had agreed that formal education would be a waste of money, as she would be married in due course where cooking, baking bread, sewing, laundry and other domestic duties would take up her time. If she were to be lucky and marry well she would still have to oversee such domesticity. In any case, she already had a fair hand and spent too much time reading.

"See how much time you'll have for reading then," I warned her grimly.

To be fair, she laid aside her books when she had chores to do, and as my daughter I expected her to show willing. One day I had to press her into an errand with which I would normally have been helped by someone else. I told her to put on a bonnet and a dark shawl and come with me.

Our destination was to Balmain, a part of Sydney that I had never visited before. We hurried along with Olivia carrying the bag that I always had with me. Up to now, Mrs Gallowshell had always carried this bag. Today, I told Olivia she was laid low as her chronic backache had worsened. I muttered to myself as we scuttled along avoiding main thoroughfares and slipping through disgustingly filthy side alleys where I was much exercised to keep from dirtying my skirts. I was repeating the instructions that I had been given.

"Keep up, keep up", I exhorted my daughter.

I could see that she struggled to do so, getting cross with me for bringing her on this errand. We stopped at a dirty side door where my furtive knock had to be repeated before it was cautiously opened a crack, then opened more to let us in.

"Who's this?" demanded a woman who resembled Baba Yaga in one of Olivia's books.

"My daughter."

The woman raised a lamp, saying doubtfully, "She's very young."

"Old enough to assist. I've no-one else at present."

I spoke sharply, feeling guilty already at drawing Olivia into this part of my life. After a moment's hesitation she turned and went back into a foetid room where a pale, listless, young woman, who scarcely seemed much older than Olivia, lay on some ragged blankets. I sent the woman away with Olivia to get hot water, but even so, she had to see what I was doing. She thought at first that I was assisting at a birth, but the true nature of what I had to do shocked her.

As we journeyed back I stopped at a crossing where we were completely alone.

"Now listen carefully. You are not to say anything to anyone about what you have just seen. Do you understand?"

Olivia nodded, her eyes wide.

"No, don't just nod. Say yes."

"Yes."

"Right. Let's get back. We have been out taking some exercise and taking the air. Do you understand?"

"Yes."

Chapter 14

Mr Pip Pirrip

I did meet Pip Pirrip when he came to Sydney some time after poor Abel Magwitch went to England. I say 'poor' because I pitied him in his obsession with his protégé. He was certainly not poor in possessions and land. I knew though that when Magwitch faced that lad, whom he had helped in England, there was every likelihood that the lad would be horrified that a transported convict was his benefactor. Abel had secretly raised him from the lowly state of being a blacksmith to be a gentleman. How often had I seen this same tragedy played out in families here, where honest, but transported, men had raised children who had turned from them, despising them. And it seemed that the more that the original felon worked to benefit his child or his children, the further they wished to push him away. I knew cases where soon after the death of a hard-working, loving father, his offspring had changed their names and denied all knowledge of their true parentage.

Mind you, this is but human nature and "twas ever thus", as my own mother was wont to say. I often fretted in the night, secretly worried that my children would not want to be known as those of a common soldier and a transported felon. You really cannot guess the future and should not waste time trying to carry out such a fruitless activity. Get on with life. Be useful. Try not to upset too many people as you make a living. Enjoy what is granted to you. I did not share Amanda Jane's firm beliefs. I had seen too much to even consider that there could exist a good God. Some clergymen who tried to explain to me why evil existed soon lost my attention. I noticed that they never seemed to suffer and were always well dressed and well fed, unlike the poor souls whom they tried to preach to.

So, as I say, I was not impressed with Mr Pip Pirrip. Amanda Jane and Arthur were completely taken in by him as they saw him as the son that they never had. I considered that he was a namby-pamby, spoiled man, used to being indulged and ready to suck upon a teat if it was made available to him. That teat was provided by Arthur, who found him a simple job that scarcely took any of his limited talents to hold on to it. Actually, I thought he was still a boy, having been kept as such by Abel's hard-earned money.

I was both surprised and then impressed when he went prospecting for gold. I thought that maybe he had some backbone after all. Maybe that chap Edward Hargreaves, the one who found all the gold and went to London to meet the Queen, had stiffened him up. He often went to the Spens household where they liked to hear his racy talk over the dinner table. Pip particularly enjoyed his company. Of course, finding that he was no longer welcome at Althorp House when Arthur and Amanda died made Pip think that he ought to do something for himself like Edward instead of sponging off others all his life. Now I liked Edward Hargreaves. Lots of people laughed at him, especially when he built that big house of his, all made of Cedar wood, at Norah Head. But at least he made a go of things. I think most of those gentry who disliked him were secretly envious, specially the ones that simply inherited estates. There's nothing finer than to look round what you have produced by your own labour and be proud of it.

It didn't surprise me in the least when I heard that Pip had been ousted from his comfortable billet. He only had it because Sir Arthur pulled the necessary strings. It was Sir Arthur Spens' relatives who threw him out of Althorp House, of course. They, knowing that they had a cuckoo in that particular nest, seized the first opportunity to get rid of it. I would have loved to have been there to see his face. Then, sitting alone in my back parlour of the shop with some of the mementos that my husband had collected, I had a change of heart. I too had been left alone so knew the pain that accompanied that state. I told Toby and Lizbeth that I was going out and, putting on an old bonnet, and my oldest shawl, I took a cab down to the docks. Badger had told me that Pip had obtained a place on the Speyside that was due to sail shortly with many forty-niners.

I told the cab driver to wait and was gratified to see him produce a feedbag for his broken-down nag, not because I felt anything for his horse, but because it meant that he was likely to wait as I had instructed him. As I went round the various drinking places several men clutched at my skirts in an attempt to accost me, taking me for what I was not. Having caught a glimpse of my face, most were scared off. The one that was too drunk to notice I beat smartly with my umbrella until he let go.

"My God!" said one man, "a man would have to be really drunk or desperate to go with you."

I stopped him as he turned away, and ignoring the rum on his breath, I asked him if he knew of any miners that were going to embark upon the Speyside. He pointed to a small group in the corner of a miserable drinking place.

"They won't have any money for you."

I walked over to them. Only one stood up, so I spoke to him in a low voice asking him whether he would like to earn some money for carrying out a service. He flinched as he saw my face, then he looked at me suspiciously, then past me to see if there was someone else with me. I drew him outside and said that my old mistress had charged me with finding someone to look out for a man and assist him at the diggings. I told him Pip's name and intimated that my mistress had a more than usual interest in his welfare. He nodded understandingly. God alone knows what he thought I meant, but it did the trick.

I described Pip, knowing that, although there would be all sorts of men on the boat, he was likely to stand out.

"I want you to make his acquaintance, and once that you have gained his confidence, stay with him until, at least he has found his feet."

I produced a small purse that made his eyes gleam.

"Put it away, I beg you. There are those here that would slit your throat for even a small amount of money. Come with me to where we can converse in some privacy."

He led me to a dirty back alley. Remembering his words about slit throats, I hesitated.

"If you are going to trust me in the future, you had better start by trusting me now."

Groping our way up some rotten stairs we reached a foul room, which even I, with all my experience of such dwellings, found totally obnoxious. There, with him sitting on what passed for a bed, he told me that his name was Antonio Magrello, but was usually called Tony. He came from Sardinia, although his ancestors had come over from Africa. He was a really solid strong man. I liked him. He had gone to California to look for gold, and was now about to do the same thing near Melbourne. His was the usual story; he had indeed found gold, and then wasted it all.

"How can I be sure that you will seek out Mr Pirrip and help him?"

"Listen. I swear upon the Holy Virgin and the life of the Pope", he said, spitting into the corner of the room.

"I spit on the devil", he explained. "He is everywhere."

He showed me his forearms, which were tattooed. I averted my eyes from the indecent pictures. He took my hand in his large brown hands with their stubby fingers and dirty broken nails, and said that despite his strength and experience, he could do with a new chum to help him, so it would be a real pleasure to seek out this Mr Pippin. The money would help to set them up properly, then, as soon as they dropped on a big one they would both be rich.

"Pirrip, Pirrip", I said.

"Yes, Pirrip."

I impressed upon him that he was in no way to tell Pip that I had spoken to him. I passed over the purse. As my mother would have said: 'nothing ventured leads to nothing gained." We went back down to the alley and then into the street. I was encouraged to see that, as I went back to my cab, he headed straight for the ship. I didn't dare follow him for fear that Pip would have seen me.

When I got back home I found Badger there, so I told him what I had done. He laughed and called me a bloody silly woman. I daresay I was, But I was a contented, stupid woman.

Chapter 14

Miss Estella Brown

When I was called into the shop, I found a soberly dressed, respectable woman with a sensible bonnet and gloves that made one think that she was at least making an effort to be a lady, even if she were not one. Her glacial manner did nothing to make me ready to assist her, but I put that down to nervousness until I got to know her better. At first I assumed that she was making the usual preliminary enquiries, but as soon as she mentioned Pip and introduced herself as Miss Estella Brown I had to change my attitude. This was no pretence colony lady. This was the real thing. Do you know, I almost did a bob! As time went on and I learned of her real origins I did not change my opinion of her. To be fair she was not the easiest of women to deal with; she was aloof, and in all the subsequent years that I knew her, she never really unbent. To the end, whatever her conduct, it was always carried out in the most ladylike way.

She was not in the slightest upset to find that Pip had gone prospecting. The faintest tightening of her lips, which many would have missed, indicated some emotion. She was not to reveal to me however what that emotion was. I said that he might be hard to find but if she were to ask around, someone might be able to tell her where he was digging. The word digging provoked another tightening. I asked whether she needed any help but her reply that Mrs Caroline Chisholm was assisting her made me sure that she would be successful. I knew that that particular lady was a formidable person who had struck terror in many a man's breast. No one would stand in the way of her finding Pip.

When she came back to Sydney we heard how Pip had started a business with a son of a tailor, John Adam. It prospered, not from Pip's efforts, but because John Adam was a determined man who was ready to ride roughshod over any and all who stood in his way. Pip unashamedly used all his previous acquaintances that he had made when working for Sir Arthur to get business. Not that that was so difficult. Everyone in the fields was so mad to dig out gold that they ignored the gold of selling stores to the miners. I thought that I detected a note of wistfulness in Estella's remarks about Pip. I suppose, as she had come all the way to Australia to find him, she had expected something other than the cool welcome that she got. She never confided in me, but Olivia and she became friendly, if that is not too strong a word for the way in which they went about together. Mrs Chisholm kept them both occupied, and I was quite pleased at this turn of events, as I wanted my Olivia to be more outgoing. Up to now she had buried herself in her books and showed no sign of being interested in attracting a suitable young man. She still assisted me, but gradually I tried to do the work on my own. I was worried that she might bring down on her head the wrath of the establishment instead of onto mine.

We both listened to Estella's accounts of the goldfields, including the hilarious story of John Adam's infatuation with Lola Montez. I could see how he had been ensnared by her, having seen her myself in Sydney before she went to entertain the diggers. She appeared at the Royal Victoria Theatre. I read all about her and her scandalous goings-on in various newspapers beforehand and that whetted my appetite to see her. Of course, I knew that she was an out and out fraud. She pretended to be all sorts of things, but so frequently changed her story that it was obvious that she tailored it to suit the circumstances of the moment. Nevertheless, she was exciting.

I saw much more of Estella when Adam and Pirrip opened an office in Sydney. It was at this time that she worked most with Mrs Chisholm, drawing Olivia into her activities. Mrs Chisholm had first established a Female Immigrant Home, and later, she also had a scheme going for female emigrants from England. So, as you might imagine, she needed all the help she could muster. I saw Estella once with a group of these bedraggled young women in the docks. They had just arrived and it was obvious that Estella's imperious manner was not resented in the slightest. They followed her like ducklings following their mother. She escorted them with their pitifully small bundles to one of Mrs Chisholm's shelters. Some looked around boldly, occasionally catching some fellow's eye, but most kept their heads down as they scurried along enjoying having someone in control in this strange new world.

I had heard plenty of criticism of Caroline Chisholm. There were no shortage of jokes about the way in which she dominated her husband, and her energy and activities were seen by many as a way to make herself more important. So what? Lots of people did quite useful things, and did it matter if they puffed themselves up as a result, if in the process some poor souls were better cared for?

Estella intrigued me. She was not a simple person. Many women would have been broken by finding out that their mother had been tried for murder, found guilty and then had to give up their child to save themselves and the child. Outwardly she seemed strong, but inwardly, I thought that she was fragile. I measured her against myself. Who else? She turned to strong characters like Mrs Chisholm and John Adam. I, on the other hand, having at one time everyone's hand against me, drew on my resolve to survive.

Chapter 15

The Last Time

I had decided that the time had come to leave my work for others to take on, when a pale, rather thin girl asked for a copy of "The Adventures of a Watch". I asked her if she was sure that that particular book was the one that she wanted. Would another suit? She knew what to say, for she cried uncontrollably when I said that I could not help her.

"Oh! You must, you must! I'm desperate. I was told that you are my only hope."

I should have been more aware of the fact that she was employed in the theatre for I found later on that she was considered to be a brilliant actress. Olivia, seeing the familiar bag, asked me not to go.

"You're really too old for this game. Leave it for someone younger."

"You?"

"No. I will not go any more. I'm sorry for these girls, but it's too dangerous. Not only if one dies but if you get caught."

"I haven't been, I won't be. I'm careful."

"So was Louisa Ford. Look what happened to her."

"Someone blew on her."

"How can you be sure that someone won't do the same for you?"

Olivia, exasperated, lost her normal calmness. She said no more, but by banging the door shut behind her as she left, she told me how upset she was. I finished preparing my bag.

The address that I had been given was in an area of town that I had never set foot in before. I was used to a much less well-swept street than this one. This one even had paving stones. The door, when I came to it was nicely painted in dark blue and sported a well-polished lion's head knocker. I used it and almost before my double knock faded the door was opened by a maid.

" I have the book that is wanted."

The usual phrase seemed to confuse her. She looked behind her as if seeking guidance. Something was wrong. I turned to go.

"Wait."

A matronly woman appeared, beckoning me in. I felt even more strongly that something was not right. Where was the girl?

She spoke to the maid:

"It's all right Effie,"

Effie bobbed obediently and went back in looking at me somewhat strangely.

"Come in please."

She stood aside smiling, but catching a glimpse of a dark figure, a man, inside in the shadows, I turned away. As I did so the woman caught hold of my sleeve. I pulled away. She held on.

"Don't go."

I tugged harder, and then I gasped as she let go of my sleeve and grasped my arm viciously. This was too much. Using my other elbow I caught her a sharp blow and heard her cry out as she fell onto me. Knowing now that something was really wrong, I turned back to face her and as she rose I swung my bag catching the side of her head with a satisfying thump. She grunted in pain her hair tumbling down around her face, my blow having loosened her pins. Now I knew I had to move fast. I trotted off and was at the end of the street when I was knocked flat. I lay there, stupidly thinking only of the indignity of my position. Some one hauled me up and wrenched my bag from my hand.

At least they washed my hand, the one that I had used to break my fall. I could tell that it was badly bruised. An older woman than I would probably have a broken wrist as a consequence. The fall had driven grit into my palm, which was bleeding. They bound it up. 'They' were the matronly woman that I had struck and a corpulent man, probably the one that had been in the shadows. He was not the man that had jumped upon my back and brought me down. He had slipped away once I had been dragged back into the house dazed and bleeding.

"We know who you are. Now we need to know more about and your companions."

Having tended to my cuts and given me a cup of tea they waited. I said nothing. My mother always said that, 'the least said the soonest mended', was a good motto.

"Tell us who you work with."

Again I maintained my silence. I ignored the tea.

"Come now, we can have you taken up for assault. You served Mrs Finnbarr grievously. Ain't you sorry about that? Come now, be sensible, tell us what we want to know."

This was interesting. No mention of a charge to do with what I thought I had been coming here to do. They held up my bag. It was open and empty. I looked beyond it to a beautiful polished walnut table upon which its contents were laid out. The corpulent man, red in the face now with exasperation at my silence, pushed at the books. I said a silent thanks to Olivia, the first person that I had exasperated this day, for reminding me of little Louisa Ford and by so doing making me cautious. No one spoke. If they thought that I was going to be the one to break the silence they were much mistaken.

The maid, Effie, came in to the room. She said nervously:

"Please ma'am, there's a cab at the door for a Mrs O'Brian."

They both looked at each other. A young man sporting a top hat, which he neglected to remove, came in and said:

"And I'm here to take Mrs O'Brian home."

He offered his arm as if I was a lady and I stood, knocking over the cup of tea that soaked into the expensive Turkey rug. I looked at Mrs Finnbarr whose hair, now once again recaptured into submission by her hairpins, and held by a jet comb, was drawn back showing the weal that I had raised on her face. I watched her face as I deliberately stood upon the teacup. It grew red with suppressed anger as we both heard the delicate china crack. A childish act I know, but so satisfying!

I gathered up the books and the bag and took the young man's arm. In the cab I was told that Effie, unknown to the Finnbarrs, had sent a boy running to my shop. Toby had sought help from John Adam and this was the result. I was glad he had gone to John rather than Pip. Pip would never have been so decisive.

"So you work for Adam and Pirrip?"

The young man smiled, smoothed his moustache, but said nothing. Instead he patted my hand. It still hurt but despite the pain I smiled back.

"Quite right too."

He was right. The least said.....

Olivia inspected my hand. We didn't talk about the books that she had placed in my bag to replace my instruments, and I didn't ask how Toby had known to go to John. I was relaxed about that. She was right too. There comes a time when a daughter knows better than her mother, and it's a wise mother who is prepared to accept that fact. Unfortunately, I was never in that position with regards to my own mother, so I was never able to say what my mother would have thought about that. Knowing her though, I'm sure that she had some adage to cover that situation.

Chapter 16

Lola Montez

I said earlier, when we were so entertained by Estella's account of John's infatuation with Lola Montez, that I had seen Lola in Sydney before she went to Melbourne. I did not go to the theatre by myself. That would have been much too forward. I needed a respectable group so that I could be part of it. Naturally, I could have simply gone, but in so doing I would have demonstrated a most unladylike attitude. It was beginning to be more important too, to maintain my position, even if it was simply that of a small shopkeeper.

Mrs Leckie needed little persuasion from me to go to see "La Grande Horizontele." at the Royal Victoria Theatre. Her husband agreed to take us once I showed him the Sydney Morning Herald where the review of her performance was set out in salacious detail. I had to get Olivia to read it, as neither Mary Leckie nor Abraham Leckie was great readers. Many might consider that a mother should try to shield her daughter from what goes on in the world. I have always taken the opposite view; the more that you know, the more you are prepared for the difficulties of life. As my mother was wont to say: "Forewarned is forearmed." In any case, reading about those follies that mark out other people's lives might help a young woman to avoid similar situations.

Olivia began by reading out loud that the newspaper thought that Lola Montez's performance was:

'The most libertinish and indelicate performance that could be given on the public stage'

She went on to read a description of the spider dance that Lola performed that was set out in such detail that the writer only succeeded in inflaming everyone's interest in actually seeing such a performance. There were details about her frame (by which we supposed they meant her body), her underwear, skirts and ankles. Mr Leckie's face suffused with a red blush as he listened, not with shame, but with desire. We knew that when Lola Montez first appeared at the Royal Victoria Theatre that business had been slow. It certainly picked up once this review appeared! What I did not tell the Leckies was that a much less flamboyant piece was to be performed on the night that we were to go to the theatre. It was the only night that we could get seats. The night that she was to repeat her spider dance was completely sold out.

Mary Leckie had been on my boat, though we never talked about it. An unspoken agreement existed that those days were past. I don't why she was transported, and she never enquired about my crime. A few other women that we both knew were thoroughly depraved, and despite their protests that they had no other choice than crime, I knew that they had a natural bent to take anything that was left unattended. I know what I saw, and I saw these women steal; they were thieves. So was Abraham, in his time. Now he passed himself off as a successful businessman. In reality he was no more than a trader. He looked for people who had a surfeit of things, bought them, and then sold them on at a much greater profit. I suppose you could say that he was still stealing, but I leave such nice distinctions to philosophers and politicians.

Both he and Mrs Leckie took care with their appearance, carefully modelling themselves on those inhabitants of Sydney who considered themselves better that common folks. Mind you, from what I heard many of these who considered themselves my betters had less claim to that status than they would have us believe. The things I overheard in my shop from supposedly respectable persons about other supposedly respectable persons.......

We all took our places in the theatre. We had laid out some money as we did not wish to be downstairs, and as we looked around, Abraham said the theatre would rival any in England. I was in no position to judge. I simply thought the whole building was magnificent. I'm afraid though that I did not totally enjoy the performance. I am sure that Lola Montez was more than adequate in her role. Everyone else swaggered around spouting long speeches that sounded as magnificent as the building that we sat in. However, just as I could admire the building without understanding the complexity of its construction, I did enjoy the spectacle without truly comprehending what was going on. Olivia loved it. So, apparently, did Mrs Finnbar who I espied on the other side of the house. Olivia explained later on, as we walked home, that Lola Montez had deliberately surrounded herself with third-rate actors and actresses in order to shine against their dullness. She had read about this and knew that this was so.

While Olivia was explaining this to me I was distracted, for I had seen amongst the players my pale-faced crying girl. I had no doubts that it was her. It was the way she held her head. No wonder she had fooled me. Only Olivia's intervention had saved me from a terrible mistake. I pressed Olivia's arm that was linked in mine. She looked at me in surprise.

"Are you all right Mama?"

I sniffed away a tear.

"It was so moving."

Mrs Leckie snorted. I glared at her, and we all continued in silence. At home, having parted from the Leckies, Olivia wanted to know why I had been upset. I told her about seeing Mrs Finbarr and the pale girl. It reminded me that I hadn't asked her about Effie, the maid. Why, I wanted to know, did she send a boy to the shop? Olivia told me that Effie's sister had been 'assisted' by me in the past, and so wanted to help me. I thought about Effie. I asked Olivia whether she resembled her sister. It troubled me that I could not bring to mind a face. Olivia said that they were totally unlike each other, both having different fathers. Despite this they were very close, supporting each other in a town where it was important to do so. Effie was a maid in service, as her mother had been in the past. Her sister was now married, having risen above her trouble, thanks to my ministrations. I was so pleased to hear this. I, or at least, people like me who assist young girls, are the target of truly offensive attacks. I understand the ethical stance that such people take in attacking my work, but they forget that there is often another ethical dimension to the situation. My mother would very often say that there were always two sides to every story. I think she would agree today, were she alive, that there might be many sides rather than two.

Chapter 17

Another Pip

Olivia called me into the shop. A soberly dressed man, quite sturdy, whose face was as battered as mine, stood there looking around him. I examined his clothes and determined that this was some workman. Olivia said that he was looking for a Jane Alambard. I said nothing, waiting for him to speak. He showed me a piece of paper, and on it I read that it was a letter to introduce Phillip Gargery, lately of Hythe in Kent, England. Apart from Hythe I made nothing of it until I bethought me of the time that Pip Pirrip had gone back to England, seemingly to seek out those who had care of him before Magwitch had paid for him to become a gentleman.

"Are you the son of those who cared for Mr Pip Pirrip? I asked bluntly. He face lit up as he said:

"So you do know him."

"Maybe we do, but who you are we are yet to be told."

"My name is Phillip Gargery, sometimes called Pip Gargery, and I am indeed the son of Joe and Biddy Gargery who, as you so rightly seem to know, acted as Pip Pirrip's parents when his own mother and father died. Both my parents are also gone to their rest now, so I am quite alone in the world. With no possibility of advancement in England, where only the idle rich and their sons and daughters are successful, I decided to try my luck in a new country where I

91

hoped I might find employment and a better state of affairs than I left in England. I have a letter to show who I am. I was told that Mr Pip Pirrip would be able to assist me. Of course, I am ready to work", he added proudly.

"I am not here to beg, just to require some assistance until I do find suitable employment."

I told this Mr Gargery that at the present time Mr Pirrip of Adam and Pirrip, was away on business in New Zealand.

"We do expect his return, but as you will know, much depends upon the weather when it coms to ships."

His face showed his disappointment. Just at that moment Estella Brown came in, and, as she loosened her bonnet strings, I appraised her of the name and circumstances of our visitor. She immediately offered him her hand and said warmly how very pleased we were to see him, and that of course we would assist him. With no further word to me she took it on herself to take him round to Pip's lodgings where he was installed and made comfortable.

When Pip did come home it was to find that he had lost the regard of Estella, because of his long absence abroad, but gained the acquaintance of a young man who was to cause us much trouble. This young man was, in my opinion, everyone's idea of a blacksmith. Big-boned, brawny, especially in his chest and shoulders, he stood a full five-foot and more. We were to discover in due course that had a brain to match that brawn, a temper and a leaning towards violence that he assuaged by fighting as a prizefighter.

Chapter 18

Warts and All

"No, he has to give me the silver."

I gave the coin back to Mrs Briggs. She gave it to little Arturo who went to put it into his pocket.

"No, give it to Mrs O'Brian. Give it to Aunty Jane."

Looking at me doubtfully, he frowned and passed the coin into my hand. I felt the roughness of the warts as he did so. I pulled out a hair from my head and wrapped round the warts, then I led him into the garden by his smooth hand, where I buried the hair, having taken it from his hand.

" It's gone, and they will soon be gone too." I intoned.

Mrs Briggs had followed us out, so I let them both out by the side gate. He ran off and she thanked me and went off too. Returning to the kitchen, I put the silver coin in with the others. I had quite a collection now. It was essential that they were kept safe to prevent a return of the warts.

Olivia mocked me as she said that she did not believe in all that hocus pocus. She said that even if my great grandmother was burned as a witch that didn't mean that I had special powers.

"Mock all you like. Just answer me this. Has anyone ever come back to say it didn't work?"

"No, because they go away naturally anyway."

"Maybe that is so. But still no-one has returned yet to ask for their money back."

"Of course not. They don't wish to look silly at believing all your nonsense."

Jamie broke in to say:

"We are never going to be a progressive country if we continue to believe in magic. It's bad enough that the blacks worship trees and go walking off into the wilderness when the fancy takes them. We should be putting all that behind us. My father would never have gone along with such superstitious nonsense."

"Your father believed in a form of magic."

This left Jamie open-mouthed with disbelief.

"Back in seventeen something or other, not long after we, that is to say, convicts, came to this country, a soldier used convicts to put on a play."

"I've heard about that. Wasn't it an officer?"

"Yes, Olivia, it was. He thought that if convicts were to put on a production of 'The Recruiting Sergeant' it would change their behaviour. It did too. It also began to open people's eyes to the fact that convicts were more than felons. In short, something magical began to happen."

"You think it magical that people began to treat everyone the same?"

"Knowing what people are like, don't you think so?"

Chapter 19

Trouble at a Ball

With the opening of some grand building, it might have been the Town Hall, I misremember which one for so many buildings were being thrust up at that time, a grand ball was arranged to celebrate it. Olivia urged me to go with her, and as I was never loath to attend such functions, I most readily agreed, particularly as John was going too and would pay for us all. I know that that sounds venal, but truly John was awash with money as his business was doing so well. His move into railways had been particularly opportune, and there was not one that was being constructed but his firm had contracts in it.

I liked the way that everyone mixed together with no-one bothering who you were, or who you had been in the past, as long as you could dance. Of course I knew that I was tolerated because Olivia, an attractive young woman, was so welcome. And I knew that being escorted by one of the richest men in New South Wales helped people considerably to overlook what many of them would have deemed an interloper. I was so pleased that such blindness on their part enabled me to enjoy myself.

John used these occasions to be seen and to talk with other businessmen. I kept well away from these discussions, so, whilst I was being escorted back to my seat by a young man who by asking me to dance hoped to move onto Olivia in due course, I only heard the raised voices and saw a confusion of movement in the distance. The sound of breaking glass and some angry sounding voices made me stand up, but I am too short, so I sent Phillip Gargery, who was sitting silently at my side, to discover what was happening. He had been there along with Estella whose dress, I might say, would have not disgraced the Governor's wife. I had a premonition that it was something to do with John.

Phillip Gargery pushed his way through the melee, his height and weight giving him an advantage. I daresay the fact that many recognised the man that had laid out the Tasmanian Devil assisted his passage. He soon returned with the news that John and Pip had fallen out, exchanged insults, and Pip had gone stalking off in a huff.

"Pip has gone now, and we must too, for John's shirt is ruined. Red wine stains so."

When John joined us his face was almost as red as his shirt. He ignored us, and taking Estella's arm, he led her away. We could tell from the way that he spoke and his frowns that he was still very angry. One or two of the firm's employees (I said that everyone mixed together, didn't I?) were present, and while the men smiled knowingly, the women's smiles were more sympathetic. I heard someone say 'drink' and the rest of the comment was swallowed up by the music, which started up at that very moment.

Looking distraught, the young man who thought that he was going to dance with my Olivia escorted us to where Phillip Gargery had gone to fetch our carriage. He stood there, the very image of the sort of respectable young man that I hoped would be her husband. I know that I married a common soldier, and I'm not ashamed that I did, but you want more for your children, don't you?" Jamie was not showing any signs that he had found the right girl either. I felt so sad as we left the main hall and the music diminished behind us. We went into a warm black night with a glorious blaze of stars that underlined the ingloriousness of two grown men's behaviour, who should really have known better. I could have boxed their ears. I really could.

Chapter 20

An Empty Bottle

Mrs Osmond settled herself in my easy chair with a grunt that told me that I was not the only one feeing my age. Mrs Leckie had told her to come, she said.

"Of course, I don't believe a word of it, but Mrs Leckie says that it works, so I am willing to give it a go."

I waited. Olivia looked in. I waved her away. She withdrew, shutting the door behind her quietly.

"It's Oliver. Come here Ollie, my love, and show Mrs O'Brian your hands."

Oliver came over to me and held out both hands. They were covered. I had seen worse, but not much.

"The others tease him so much, don't they darlin'? They say he's dirty and it makes him cry. He gets enough teasing without this as well."

She gave me a knowing look as I ran my hands over his curly black hair and looked into his caramel eyes. I thanked him and he went back to playing with our newly acquired cat, a good mouser, I had been assured.

"He's......?"

"Yes, and his mother died in having him, poor soul."

I didn't ask who father his was. Let sleeping dogs lie, as my mother would say. No use stirring up trouble unnecessarily. I pulled out several hairs, thinking that they were getting rather sparse. No wonder old ladies wore mobcaps. Perhaps I should get one. That would give Olivia and Jamie something to laugh at. I wrapped them around Oliver's hands, which stayed submissively in mine as I led him into our yard. I took off the hairs and whispered the usual words as I buried them in the dirt. To my intense surprise Oliver repeated what I had said perfectly. He then sang them and clapped his hands in a rhythm that altered subtly as he kept repeating what I had whispered. Eventually he stopped and looked at me solemnly.

I took him back to Mrs Osmond. I wondered if she realised that I knew of her husband and his tastes. Many did, apart from me. Badger had taken great delight in filling in all the details when he told me about Mr Osmond's trips up the river.

"There you are dear. Say goodbye to Mrs O'Brian and go to play in the yard while I speak to her.

"How much?"

It does not matter how much or little, but he has to give it to me himself."

Grumbling about silly superstitious nonsense, she called him back and gave him some silver. Singing my words softly he gave it to me and finished by saying some native words.

"Don't pay any attention to him. Come along dearest, let's get you home."

Once they had gone I looked for the bottle in which I put the coins. It was not where it was supposed to be, on the top shelf. I got a chair, and standing on it, I reached the back of the shelf where I found the bottle pushed behind some old books that Amanda Jane had brought from England, and had given me years ago. I dusted them off and got down. The bottle was empty, as I knew it would be from its weight.

Olivia's face, when I showed her the bottle told me everything.

"Why does he do it?"

"The usual."

"I thought he promised after last time."

"He did, but you know what he's like. He always promises anything and everything to anybody when he's sober. He says that it's not his fault. The other workmen are jealous of him and his skills, so they poison the ears of his employers and that means that he keeps losing his job. He's practically blacklisted now. He gets drunk; gets into fights, then employers won't even look at him. You won't tell Pip will you?"

"What about John?"

"Oh, he knows. He knows everything, but Pip goes around with his eyes shut."

" And Toby?"

"You know how it is with Toby. As long as he sees me regularly, he will do anything I ask."

I very much hoped so. Toby worried me. I knew that he liked Olivia, who could twist him round her little finger, but one day he would want more than just seeing her, what then? I dusted off the books again, they really were filthy and so old, and I remembered how Amanda Jane had told me that they had been given to her by the nuns in England who had cared for her. As they were so out of date she considered them worthless. I thought otherwise. I looked at the books. They were:

Culpeper's Pharmacopoeia Londonesis of the Royal College of Physicians; and Culpeper's work on midwifery entitled *A Directory for Midwives; or a Guide for women in their conception, bearing and suckling of their children, etc.*

I determined to take them into Robertsons, the large bookstore, but finding that they had shut down and were only doing business in Melbourne, I put the books to one side and, once again, forgot about them.

Chapter 21

Pip a Hero

I had to change my opinion of Pip considerably. I had already modified it somewhat following his time in the goldfields, where, after Tony Magrello's death, he had matured. But now I learned that he had shown courage and maturity in a situation that would have tested the bravest man. We had all read in the newspapers about the way in which a young woman had became involved in the rescue of the passengers and crew of the S.S. Georgette in Calderup Bay. This brave young woman and a stockman rode into the sea on their horses as the steamship was breaking up and passengers were scrambling pell-mell into the lifeboats. Between them they rescued many, although some were drowned. These survivors were taken to Wallcliffe where the family cared for them. She was described as "Western Australia's Grace Darling".

When I had read this story in the newspaper I had no idea that Pip had been on the ship and had been one of those who had been rescued. Then one of Olivia's friends, Elaine Pomeroy, who worked in John and Pip's office in Sydney, told Olivia that not only had he been rescued, but that he had acted heroically! Elaine's quick acid wit and humour more than made up for her lack of looks. In short she was a plain dumpy young woman who knew that she was always going to be passed over in favour of such attractive women as Olivia and Lizbeth were. Why was she Olivia's friend? It was the old story: Elaine was taken along when Olivia went out as a contrast to Olivia. Young men who wished to dance with Olivia had to dance first with Elaine.

Elaine knew that Pip had been on a tour of the firm's offices, which had meant that he had been booked on the SS Georgette. What really brought the whole matter to light, however, was a survivor whom Pip had paid for to return to Sydney, who came to the offices to thank him. Elaine had taken this man to Pip, who having accepted his thanks and shaken his hand, had sworn Elaine to secrecy. Apparently, according to this man, Pip had acted in an exemplary manner, saving others without regard for his own life until the ship had nearly foundered. Only then had he cast himself into the boiling surf to be saved himself by "Western Australia's Grace Darling".

Of course, Elaine, silly girl, had been unable to keep this to herself, but what was more interesting was that the man who told Elaine of Pip's bravery, said that a young woman was giving a monologue performance at a little theatre in Sydney about the episode. She too had been rescued.

I had heard vaguely about this woman, but had not given it much attention. Now, urged on by Olivia and Elaine I determined to go to a performance. The show was advertised as:

" The Truly Heroic and Shocking Story of the Fateful End of the Steamship Georgette."
Introduced by Maria De Lasseps

Who suffered herself in this cruel episode, but is willing to put aside her pain and anguish to bring to her public the truth.

We took our seats, just the three of us, as we wished to respect Pip's desire to remain an anonymous hero. The curtains swished back, and there, in the newly installed limelight, a young woman stood in a dramatic pose. We all fell silent. She lifted her right arm, pointed to the wings where someone made storm and wave sounds, and as they died away she began her story. For the next thirty or so minutes she held our attention, painting with words an unforgettable picture. We were there, suffering with the crew and passengers. We felt the strain of trying to launch the lifeboats; we experienced the horror of watching people perish; we suffered the agony of not being able to help those dashed to their deaths. We groaned, and then we applauded as she came to the end of part one of her powerful presentation. She curtsied and the curtains slid back and the limelight went off.

I was somewhat taken aback when Elaine immediately arose and bade us follow her, for she did not go to the front of the theatre, which I now saw was rather more shabby than it had seemed earlier, but to a side door where she spoke softly to an attendant who nodded and let us through. Seeming to know her way she led us through a gas-lit corridor that could have done with some cleaning. She knocked. A voice asked who was there. When Elaine replied, the door swung open and we all trooped in. I felt as if I was in someone's idea of a Turkish harem. The corridor might have been grubby and in need of a cleaning, but this room shone.

A young woman seemingly dressed all in veils said that Maria De Lasseps was pleased to receive us, but as she needed to preserve her voice for part two, asked our forgiveness if she didn't speak. Before I could ask what was the point of our being there then, she asked us if we liked her part of the performance.

"What was that?"

"I was the wind and the waves; I set the tone and ambience for Miss De Lasseps performance.

"Oh!"

Her voice hardened somewhat at my response as she asked if there was any particular point to our visit. Miss De Lasseps, laid out on a chaise-longue and veiled like an odalisque, sighed theatrically and whispered:

"I must make myself available to my public."

Elaine now told both ladies how she knew someone who had been on the SS Georgette. She said that he had been a hero; only being rescued himself at the last minute. Maria De Lasseps sat up, threw back her veil and said sharply that she was not an impostor. Elaine hastened to assure her that we were sure that she had suffered, as did the others. We were, however, seeking to hear what she might know of a certain gentleman whose bravery on the ship attracted everyone's admiration. He was one of the last to escape, and gave a sum of money from his own pocket to aid those less fortunate than he.

"I know who you mean! What a hero! How noble a gentleman. What consumate delicacy in assigning to others of less noble birth than he the plebeian task of distributing alms. From the moment I saw him at the farm on the following morning he impressed me with his manly air and noble disposition."

She then fell back, saying that to be fair, she could say no more. She had to save herself for the second act. Then started up to whisper that we could, if we desired, meet her at a certain chophouse near-by after the performance. We left, agreeing to this arrangement and enjoyed the remainder of the performance before repairing to Guiseppe's.

I almost missed her entrance as I was perusing the menu. She coughed loudly, Olivia nudged me, and when Luigi Guiseppe went over to welcome her, and she had everyone's attention, she sashayed in to a gentle applause waving a languid hand.

"Please, please, no more. You are too kind. I'm supposed to be incognito to see some admirers who absolutely insisted that I come, despite my exhaustion after a performance."

As she came over to us she distributed some handbills about her show. While we had been waiting for her, Elaine told us that she was really Mary Lassy, her parents having come to New South Wales from Cardiff in Old South Wales

"They have a fried fish shop", she added. " I go there sometimes, their flathead fish is lovely."

Despite her exhaustion, Maria managed several chops, which I knew I would be paying for. She also managed to down several big glasses of wine and as she did so, became more and more garrulous. Some traces of a much less refined accent emerged in her voice as she described how Pip had indeed been a hero. She told us that when the pumps stopped everyone had to bail. Some tried to refuse. They were all given buckets, but he led them in this, setting an example. At this time the captain was simply steering for the shore for there was little else that he could safely do. With the dawn there was still no let up in the weather and all the attempts to get the pumps started again failed. They heard the ship's engine slow and then stop. It was then, as the waves threatened to overcome them, that he helped launch boat after boat. He must have been desperately tired. They all hung on to whatever they could to save themselves. He helped launch another boat. It was immediately swamped. It was then that Maria threw herself into the sea and was rescued by Grace Bussell on her horse.

Chapter 22

Reconciliation

I heard the full story from Olivia, who was used by Estella, as Estella was so very distressed, as many of us were, at the silly way that John and Pip were carrying on. Estella, unknown to John, with whom she was living, much to many a so-called lady's displeasure, asked Olivia to get an envelope to Pip. Well, Livvy went to Elaine, and gave her Estella's envelope to deliver. This was easy, for Elaine still worked at Adam and Pirrip, and it was the work of a moment to slip it onto his desk.

Livvy had said that if she were to help Estella she needed to know what was in the envelope, as she would not be party to anything underhand. It was a ticket for a box at the theatre. Estella, desperate to reconcile the men, hoped that Pip would go to the theatre where she would slip into the box once he had arrived. There she planned to appeal to his better nature to end the bitter feud. She did not dare meet him openly. Apparently John was tremendously jealous.

We never found out exactly what happened, although we did know that Pip did indeed go to the theatre and Estella joined him. We knew this as I wheedled Olivia into watching in the street to see their arrival. She said that soon after Estella went in she came out looking agitated, hailed a cab and was driven off.

For a few days we were all on tenterhooks. We all wondered if Estella's stratagem had been successful. Then Elaine, that soul of discretion, told us that the men had met. I

111

don't know how she managed it, but I would not put it past her to have listened to what should have been a private conversation, but she knew the whole of what had passed between them. Apparently, John was not well and because of this they agreed to make up their differences. A Dr Fordyce had warned John to take life at a much slower pace if he hoped to live longer.

After this the two men appeared to come to their senses to a certain degree. My mother always said however that: 'one never knew what two might do'.

Chapter 23

The Clontarf Picnic

It was a lovely March day with little puffy white clouds floating across one of Australia's perfect blue skies. Getting to Clontarf was easy as there were a number of small boats taking people to the picnic. Some went from the half circular quay straight there whilst others crossed over to Neutral Bay and came along the road to the Spit where they got a boat across to the beach where the tents were set out for the picnic. I stayed at home. Picnics I found tedious. When we first came to this land we were forced to eat outdoors, now, here we are years later choosing to go back to that primitive state.

John went with Estella and Olivia. Pip did not go. Despite their reconciliation the two men still met but infrequently. Estella was cool about the possibility of seeing royalty. Her days in London had given her ample opportunities to see princes, dukes, earls and all orders of nobility. Olivia was much more excited. She pretended that she was indifferent to the thought of mixing with a much better class of person than we usually had in Sydney, but I knew her and I knew her moods. Young Jamie and Phillip Gargery kept me company at home. John knew the Thornes and expected to join them at some time during the day. He was hoping that he and the ladies might be presented to the Duke of Edinburgh. I was confused. I thought that the son of a queen had to be a prince. I knew that the picnic was in aid of the Sailor's Home, a charity to which John had donated a considerable sum. This had enraged Phillip Gargery who wanted to know why John and Pip didn't spend such amounts on their own employees.

I later heard the whole story from Olivia and, of course, I read all about it in the newspapers. They saw the prince's arrival and heard in the distance the address that was made as he landed at the pier. How these dignitaries love the sound of their own voices. They enjoyed the bands and had a quite splendid lunch in a tent that was specially set out for that purpose. I could have gone after all! It was all very civilised. John tried to get near to George Thorne who was there with his family, but, although John is quite important, he is not so important that he can always order things the way he wishes them to be. He had to be contented with taking a seat and watching with the others.

Estella said that the sun was giving her a headache and was urging John to think about leaving, when the royal party came out to much cheering. This was the chance that John had hoped for and he made himself ready by standing up, but to his great chagrin the royal party went off in the other direction. John turned to say that he was vexed at this, when there was a noise like a firework followed by screams.

Later on everyone knew, of course, that a man had tried to shoot the prince. Then running out came George Thorne calling loudly that he had been shot too. You can imagine the frenzy of activity that now took place, and as they captured the would-be assassin (for the prince was not dead, only badly injured) he might have been put to death there and then, had the police not kept tight hold of him. John said that he was a blackguard Irishman, a Fenian. I hoped that he was simply mad. Being Mrs O'Brian might otherwise have meant my shop window being broken, or worse.

Ever since this event Olivia insists that I was there with them all. I have said repeatedly that she was mistaken; I stayed at home. For days the newspapers were full of it; how they caught hold of the assassin; how the prince was taken to be cared for by a parcel of English nurses who had been sent out to New South Wales; his recovery, and the money that was collected to build the new hospital.

Then, eventually, we had all the details of the trial of the Fenian who was found guilty and sentenced to hang. It was no more than he deserved, but Pip Gargery thought otherwise, and annoyed many with his comments about natural justice and how the nobility would all get their just deserts one day.

Chapter 24

Estella Dies

The first that we knew was when Jamie came back from inside the station to say that there had been trouble on the line. We had gone to meet John and Estella there, as they were to visit us for dinner. A coach and horses came round the old road, and as it stopped, a man stepped out and told everyone that was gathered there the news. Jamie held the horses' heads as their flanks steamed from having been driven so fast.

People pressed forward. I was pushed along, but there was so much noise that it prevented me from hearing clearly what the man was saying. I must admit my hearing had been getting worse so that didn't help. He waved for people to be quiet and I heard the word 'accident'.

An ostler took the snaffle from Jamie who crossed to where I was standing and took my arm, pulling me away.

"What did he say? What's happened? Tell me. Tell me."

"There's been an accident. The train came off the line on the new bend. They have taken them to the hospital in Sydney."

"Who? Who have they taken? Is it John? Is it Estella? Who?"

"Go back to the shop and tell Liv while I go to Sydney to find out what's happening. Go and tell Toby to see whether the station has heard of any news on the telegraph system."

He left, in the carriage that went down to Sydney using the old road. I went back to find Olivia who had heard already that something was amiss. Bad news travels fastest, as my mother always said. She was outside the new shop looking anxious with Toby behind her. I sent him to the station remarking to myself how he had aged recently. I knew that he liked Olivia and would have spoken for her if I had given him the least encouragement. It was his attachment to her that kept him in our employ, and it was at times like this that I realised how lucky we were to have someone so steadfast and true to help us. Jamming his hat over his eyes he ran off, his gait comical were it not for the seriousness of the situation.

"We didn't shut the shop. It's not good for trade if people don't find you open when you are supposed to be."

"Good girl. You're right. Let's go in."

We sat with the new stock mocking us. All our efforts to be a success, and now this! As my mother would often remind me: 'man proposes, God disposes.' A few customers came in, mostly to ask if we had heard the news. In time a red-faced Toby returned and after a drink of water and a wipe or two around his sweating head, he told us that the crash was serious, at least two dead, several hurt. One of the injured was Estella. There was no news yet of how badly she had been injured. We shut the shop and tried to eat our dinner.

The following day Jamie came back. He had found Phillip Gargery at a Labour meeting, dragged him away and went to the hospital where he knew Estella was in one of the wards. They would not let either of them in at first, as they were not relatives, so Jamie pretended that Estella was his aunt. This got him in for a few moments and he was able to sit by her bed, then an officious nurse turned him out saying that if she was upset it would set her back.

"She was so pale. I think she knew me. I held her hand for a moment before that bitch sent me packing."

I had never seen Jamie so upset. Olivia was very silent too. When we went to bed it was with a dark sensation that something awful was about to happen. The awful thing did happen, for we heard that they had to remove Estella's leg, but despite all their efforts she died. You would think that knowing now what they had learned in the Crimea war, those nurses would have been able to save her, but they didn't.

John behaved very badly, for he simply shut himself away letting others make arrangements for the funeral. So, in consequence we never heard where was to be, and when, until it was too late. Pip didn't hear either, and he thought that John had acted out of malice. I'm still not sure because both men were rivals in so many ways.

Something else came of all this. Olivia came home one day and I had never in all my born days seen her so excited. She was so lively and in such good spirits that I thought at last that some young man had caught her fancy. Maybe I was to be a grandmother after all! Jamie, for all his sweethearts, never seemed to light upon one that he really wished to marry, for all that he wanted to be seen out with them. He and Amos, his best friend, were always surrounded by young women, but I think they were too choosy by half.

Composing myself I waited after she made me sit down, only to hear that she put herself forward to be trained as a nurse. I was bitterly disappointed. I had had some experience in the past with the sort of women that were nurses, and a common, foul-mouthed, drunken lot they were too. I lost no time in pointing these facts out to my high and mighty daughter for whom no man was good enough.

"Oh! Ma," she exclaimed, "It's different now. Miss Nightingale has sent a body of trained nurses to Sydney. They wear proper uniforms and the doctors look to them to nurse their patients back to health. Did we not read how they did just that after the Prince was shot at the picnic?"

Well, I had read something about this and about the new hospital that was being built, but I didn't want a daughter of mine acting as a slavey, no matter how she would be in a grand hospital and wearing a uniform.

"Anyway", she went on. "I still have to be selected. They are strict about who they select."

This riled me. I was irked that my daughter had to be looked over as if she was some form of animal for them to select or reject her.

"I must wait for the official letter. You know Miss Nightingale has met the Queen. You can't get a better recommendation than that."

Chapter 25

Pip Pirrips' Final Inheritance

It gave me quite a turn when I heard that John and Pip had found some papers that proved that Pip really had an inheritance. I knew, you see, that Lady Amanda would never have left Pip without something. Sir Arthur was another matter. Although he regarded Pip as the son that he had never had, he was far too ready to be swayed by his relatives. They persuaded him to draw up papers that overrode Lady Amanda Jane's wishes. When they both died and Pip was turned out of Althorp House I thought that he had finally lost everything. That was why I tried to help him without him knowing.

Mind you, it was John who did all the spadework, using those lawyers of his. He was always able to put others to work on his behalf. Now he used them to find out something to Pip's advantage. They poked about in the colony's early records and found that papers had been put away in a bank. It's truly amazing what you can find if you have someone to do the ferreting that's needed. I expect that when we are all dead and gone, someone will find some dusty old papers about the early convicts and settlers that will show that we were not so bad as people made us out to be.

Both John and Pip went to a bank and there they managed to retrieve a will of Abel's, a letter from lady Amanda Jane and that very watch that I rescued from the fire along with a scrap of newsprint.

They handed over the papers to 'Beckridge and Blownding', two bloody old legal scoundrels, according to many who had had dealings with them. However, If any were able to manipulate what had been found so that it finally came out to Pip's advantage, it would be these two. I knew the daughter of Blownding for she was a clever portraitist who eventually made quite a good living from selling portraits. I sold some for her that had been ordered but not paid for. I persuaded her that she should expand her repertoire to include houses and suchlike scenes. Many well-placed families ordered these from her and she did pretty well until photography began to spread and take away her customers. That's the problem with progress; there are always losers.

So Pip finally achieved what he had always wanted to be: a gentleman of leisure. His house was a good solid one, nothing flashy, very respectable. Jamie, as a good carpenter and joiner, worked on it. So did Phillip Gargery, and by so doing managed to get enough money together and courage to ask my Olivia to marry him. I had to wait for her to make up her mind though. In the meantime, when I was over at Satis Novis one day, Pip said that he had something to show me.

It was a letter that was part of the papers that had been hid away for so long.

Dearest Pip,

When you read this, if you ever do, I shall be dead, and you should be the heir to what Arthur and I are leaving behind in this world. I say should because life is never straightforward and the litigation and grasping that I have seen in my lifetime persuades me that once Arthur and I are gone his relatives may well have won out against our wishes.

You may wonder why Arthur and I did not make it over to you when we were alive. As I write this you are making your own way quite successfully which is as it should be. I know that you are not entirely satisfied with your present employment but I am confident that in time the name of Pip Pirrip will be recognised as the name of a successful respected gentleman.

I have protected one thing along with these papers that I should like you to have. You remember that when I told you how I helped Abel how I also was under threat from Freddy, and Jane was instrumental in getting back my father's watch.

Please keep it in memory of all those people who have struggled to help you become the Australian gentleman that you are.

Amanda Jane

I read it with deep emotion. It was as if Amanda Jane was speaking to me from the past.

Chapter 26

John Adam Marries

With Estella dead, John took to going about with a veritable series of ladies, some of whom even I looked at askance. He neglected his business, and when Pip remonstrated with him he replied that he must have an heir. Pip finally severed his relationship with him breaking up the old firm. Many were rather sad to see it go and to see just **'Adams'** appear in its place. Elaine was still employed there, despite her age. She knew so much about how things worked that she was practically irreplaceable. Her tales of John's new bride and of her temper kept us all amused.

"There is no fool liken to an old one," I said once to an assembled company of us as we had a quiet time together and remembered past events.

"My mother always had a saying for all times, and that was one of her favourites."

We read about the proposed wedding in the papers, how his bride had come from Italy and had insisted on all sorts of ceremonies. We all had invitations. I still have mine as I put it behind the clock on the mantel.

We went to the wedding, where, at first, I was quite put out for I was largely ignored. Then I realised that, as I was getting older, I was becoming much less important in everyone's eyes. John did stop to speak to me, but was pulled away by his new bride who reminded me of Tony, the Sicilian, who I had asked to look out for Pip when he went to the goldfields.   It was the way she crossed herself and spat sideways muttering about eyes, not the conduct of a true lady. I asked Olivia what it all meant but she told me to hush and not cause such a fuss and draw attention to myself.   After that I went and sat in the corner, not even taking part in the dancing. The food was good though!   I told Olivia at first that I wouldn't have any, then, when she went off to dance, I tried some.   I know it was all foreign stuff, but it was quite good, so I set to and got Jamie and his pal to get me some more.

As much as anything I did it to stop them quarrelling. They were having a right time of it, and in public too.   That Amos is a funny lad, such a strange looking young man. Lizbeth and all the other girls seem to like him though.   I got him to show me round the house, which was like a palace.   He told me that it was built like an Italian palatzo.   The plans came from Italy and were based upon a famous palatzo on the coast. He did tell me the name, but I can't remember it now.

When we came back Jamie had got us some wine. The wine was all sparkly, just like the stuff that I had to produce when Amanda Jane and Arthur announced that they were to be wed. After two glasses of it I couldn't help but cry, thinking about my Jamie, how we were wed and how he died.

Chapter 27

Not a Nurse, a Bride

You would have thought that the world was coming to an end when the letter came after Olivia had been interviewed, and my God, the fuss she made about her appearance before she went off to that. It was short and not sweet. It simply said that it was regretted that Miss Olivia O'Brian was not selected. For some days our household went into mourning. It was lifted eventually when Olivia told me that she had decided to accept Phillip Gargery's proposal of marriage.

Of course, no one took any notice of what I thought. I was just Olivia's Mama, an old woman who now had to give way to the fads and fancies of the younger generation, most of who knew little or nothing of life. But, there you are, that's life these days. The young have no respect for their elders and betters. Phillip Gargery didn't even have the decency to come and ask for Olivia's hand, just assuming that I would say yes.

Ever since Phillip Gargery had been part of our household I had become increasingly uneasy about him and his conduct. I didn't expect him to act like a gentleman. He was too low born for that. I did expect him, however, to be a steady worker and to be moderate in his drinking. Naturally, I didn't expect him to give up alcohol completely. Living with Jamie, my ex-soldier husband had made me completely aware of how men take liquor and the effect it has upon them. Just occasionally he would take a drop too much. With Phillip Gargery though, it wasn't occasional. And I couldn't really take to the fact that he fought. I know it was described as a sport. I know too that many a real gentleman spoke to Phillip Gargery almost as if they were equals when he was in the ring. It wasn't a noble art as far as I was concerned. But that was the problem. No one cared about what concerned me.

Why did Olivia finally accept him? You might well ask. 'Better to save your breath to cool your broth than ask silly questions' as my mother would have advised. But maybe it wasn't that silly a question. She certainly never gave me a straight answer to anything that I asked her about the matter, despite the fact that she was my daughter, who you might have supposed owed me the respect that a daughter should show her old mother. But that's the modern generation for you.

Her trouble was that she was too pernickety. She could have had any number of suitors who were attracted to her like moths to a bright light. Some, it must be said, recoiled from her plain way of speaking about her past. She insisted that she was merely the daughter of a convict. I heard her tell a very presentable young man that were they to have children, their grandmother would be a transported felon. I was not surprised to see him no more. When I taxed her with what I had heard she first scolded me for listening, and then said that anyone who courted her deserved to know the truth. I said that her father was a common soldier who drank. Did she tell them that too? She said that she had not done so far, but would bear it in mind the next time. No wonder I felt vexed!

At least Phillip Gargery accepted us as we were. In fact he rather gloried in the idea that we were oppressed workers. I must say though that when he got onto this particular tack, I thought he spoke a great deal of rubbish. Mind you, he was not alone in that, for there were plenty who chose not to settle into regular work, preferring to fight for their rights. I noticed that many of them were Irish, a race that I was always suspicious of. They were all tinkers, horse thieves or worse. I know that I am an O'Brian, but only by marriage.

I told him that I had never heard such a lot of nonsense.

"Phillip Gargery", I said on one occasion when he had spouted a great deal of high flown words, from I know not where, for he was incapable of dreaming them up hisself, "my mother used to say: 'Handsome is …..

…as handsome does", he finished for me with a great laugh.

He was a great one for a laugh, and would turn off criticism with a great bellow of mirth.

Chapter 28

The Wedding Present

Pip Pirrip just couldn't resist having us over to his house that reminded me of Edward Hargreaves and that big house of his, all made of Cedar wood that he had built at Norah Head. Pip's house was built of stone and brick because we had any amount of men making bricks now, not like in the early days when everything had to be brought out from England. I remember Alfred Trimble telling me that he had travelled out in one boat that had used bricks as ballast. Then, once arrived, the bricks were sold to someone who used them to build something a deal more solid than they had up to that time.

This house was very like the one that was built at the same time for a butcher in Sydney who had done so well that he thought that he would have a big house like the gentry. And why not pray? His money is as good as anyone else's. I thought it best not to say this. Pip took us round as if we were being given a lecture. My legs gave out; they are not so good as they were, so I waited in his drawing room, but I was there when he gave Olivia and Phillip Gargery the present.

The present was two ornate pieces of Chinese pottery. I thought that they were quite ugly. Olivia pretended to like them for Pip's sake, but I could see from her expression that she was being polite. He seemed to think that they were extremely valuable. He gave them to the happy couple, saying:

"I got them when I was in the goldfields. I just happened to help a Celestial, a Chinaman, who was so grateful that he insisted that I take them. They apparently have some symbolic value. If you look at the decoration it would tell some sort of story related to the dragons and phoenix that are depicted round the edge of each piece. They are extremely heavy so be careful as you lift them."

Phillip Gargery hefted them off the mantle. He grunted in surprise at their weight. Once we got them home they were put away and I never set eyes on them again.

Chapter 29

He's Gone

Olivia thought that she could hide the truth from me, but I knew from the way she tied her apron and pulled at the edges to straighten it, that she had something not so nice to tell me. Normally she would simply put on her apron and begin work.

"He's gone Ma. Run off because he is in trouble."

I really didn't want to hear more. I knew who she was talking about. I always knew something like this would happen, but no one listens to me any more. Still I waited just in case she wanted to tell me the rest of the story. She didn't say another word. In the end I got the whole story as Toby told Lizbeth. Just because I'm a little hard of hearing now they think I can't hear them, as they whisper together.

He told her how he got so drunk that he got into a fight and killed someone. Now, I know that I'm an old woman and I don't understand the modern world with its trains and suchlike, but something didn't make complete sense. It may have been the way in which Toby told Lizbeth. I sensed a certain pleasure, a feeling that something had been engineered, brought about, rather than just happened. That was it! He might have been describing something that had been performed, something seen on a stage. How could he have seen all he described if he had just happened upon it? He must have been there from the beginning.

I know people think that I'm a funny old thing what lives in the past, but I'm sharp enough to question something that doesn't seem quite right. I suppose that I have heard too many villains in the past spinning their yarns that contain just enough truth to persuade the listener that the whole thing is the complete truth. Some of them have been past masters of the art of skewing the facts. Badger was one such. My God! Couldn't he just tell the tale? Being in the army was the school where he honed that skill to perfection. My Jamie was not too bad at it either! Sergeant Majors like to hear what they want to hear, he used to say.

Chapter 30

The shop Fails and Olivia at Parramatta

Why anyone should think that running a bookshop is easy I have no idea. I certainly struggled, even with help. The problems just mount up. So when Olivia told me that we were in trouble I was not in least part surprised. Apparently it was Toby who looked at all the figures and persuaded her to give it up. I knew my Livvy well enough to know that she would have some plan or other to see us through.

Sure enough she had worked it all out. We were to move from the shop and leave Toby to take it over, as he seemed to think that he could make a go of it. He would give us something for the goodwill and this would be enough to pay our rent for a while. Olivia had secured a position in the girl's school in Parramatta and this would pay enough to maintain us both. Jamie would have to seek lodgings near to where he would be employed. The contracts that we had to supply bookcases to the government had meant that he had got a good reputation and so had a secure position, as secure as anything can be, that is.

We would have to say goodbye to Lizbeth, but she had known for some while that this was a possibility. Toby was firmly of the opinion that he could not afford to employ her. Our goodbyes were muted, as we knew that we would be seeing Lizbeth, for she too had secured employment nearby.

Things didn't work out as well as Livvy wanted them to. Jamie had to go away somewhere to do with his work. All these changes. I could hardly keep up with them.

But that Mrs Kaye, she was nice. When my Livvy came home and told me about her I knew at once that she was a lady. The way she asked after me, and the trouble that she took to help Livvy and me, you wouldn't believe.

I knew from her accent that she was from England, and from what she let slip I could tell that her Ma and Pa were cultured people. The fact that she had worked in Australia meant nothing to me to distract from her gentility. Many a lady had to descend to work when they fell on hard times. She spent quite a whiles with me before she said that she had obtained a place for me in a home. And even then she would sit with me and I would tell her about my early days in the colony. It was for Livvy to make the final decision, of course, and I was sure that as we had so little money that would be the end of that.

You can imagine the surprise when that old bit of china that Pip had given us turned out to be so valuable. I say the china was valuable, but it was what it contained that really set us back. My Livvy sat and looked at it for some while before wrapping it up and taking it off. And, you should just have seen her face when she came back with all that money!

I have never in all my born years set eyes upon such a sum. I had to pick it up and run it through my fingers to be sure that it was real. It was enough for our needs, and for Livvy to send some to Jamie. A message came back to thank us and to say that as how he and Amos Bulstode were going to take it and set up in partnership as joiners. Naturally, I was disappointed. I was pleased too, but you do want to see your children about you.

Where Phillip Gargery had gone I had no idea. When they had that dreadful to-do over Toby, who had such an awful accident that Livvy has said I must not talk about, he went away. He had done that before. I only saw him briefly, but I knew him, despite the beard. It's funny, but I can't really remember much about that time. Livvy says that I had to have medicine, but for what? My mother was wont to say.....but I forget now what she used to say, and Livvy says that it doesn't matter any more.

Chapter 31

Cast Off

Honestly, just because I could no longer manage the stairs and forgot a few things, and just you tell me who remembers everything all the time, they thought that I could be put here to look at the walls all day. I know, I know, they push us out to sit on the veranda, but only when they remember to. And, that's another thing, they are all black girls who look after us. Not that I've anything against them. Some of them are very nice. I do admit that business with the candle was a real fright to everyone. Just because I did it once doesn't mean though that I shall be doing it every day, does it?

I do miss my Jamie. They tell me lies here, saying that he is dead, but I still see him, sometimes in my dreams, I admit, but at other times he's as real to me as if we had just been married. So how can he be dead? He might be dead to them, just because they don't have my gifts, but to me he's here with me, and always will be. I sometimes see him in uniform and I am so proud of him. I have to admit that I'm proud that he chose me.

Mrs Kaye is very nice to me. She wanted me to call her Emilie, but I think that I shall continue to treat her as the lady that she so clearly is. Not like that bitch that John's married. From all accounts he's being led a fine dance by her, and no mistake. Just because she comes from Italy!

As I said, Mrs Kaye is very nice; she has a simple way of showing how she cares about us poor souls. I often wonder where Livvy gets the money to pay for me to stay here. Livvy says that I know very well where the money comes from, and sometimes I have a certain feeling that I do. It's all bound up with dreams that I have. All my laundry is done, and all the food, such as it is - why everything is always cut up I shall never know - is provided free. But as my mother would say: 'Never look at Greeks if they want to give you something.'

The other day, I can't remember exactly when, she, that is Mrs Kaye, was with me and I could see that she was troubled about something. As my mother would say: 'A trouble shared is a trouble halved', so I took the liberty of taking her hand in mine and said:

"Tell me what it is that is troubling you."

You would have thought that my hand was a burning coal, for she snatched her hand away and gave me such a look. She wanted to know who had been talking to me. I told her no one. That's one of the things about this place; people just ignore you. Then a look came over her and I thought that she was a'going to cry. But no, instead she sets herself down beside me and swears me to keep secret what she has to say, and I shall do so. So far, I have never yet betrayed a secret nor broken a promise.

At my age nothing much shocks me, but I must admit what she had to say shook me. How could she? Her own brother? I kept silent until she had finished. She waited for me to make some comment. I still kept silent until she said:

"What do you think I should do?"

I said that I did not know what she *should* do. I could however suggest what she *might* do. She leaned back apparently satisfied with that answer. I then said that apart from the easing that telling me provided her, were she to write all this down and give it to someone to read she might find that helped soothe her somewhat. She nodded. She got up, thanked me and we never spoke again about this matter.

The end

Part two

The Magwitch Effect

Phillip Gargery's Story

Only a Blacksmith

Chapter 1

Leaving England for a Better Land

The crowd cheered. The blood from my cut face and nose ran freely. My opponent, a grizzled, old professional grinned at me. I closed with him anxious to land a blow but he pulled me to his sweaty, stinking body, and as he did so he opened his mouth to reveal blackened stumps of teeth and whispered:

"Keep it going lad. You're a game one. They like you, and if I go down we can share takings."

I was fighting The Black Butcher for a small purse. Afterwards I would be allowed to take my hat round to augment it. Sure enough a blow from me sank my opponent who stayed down until he was counted out. The takings were not that large, but as I sat with him and we shared them they seemed enough for what I had in mind. I staunched the flow of blood and hoped that my face was not too battered. It was certainly not as well worn as my erstwhile opponent. We shared some ale and a pie that could have been made when I was a lad. Luckily I still had most of my teeth.

"You're a reet handy young fella sithy. We could make a mint. They love to see an old pro like me felled by a youngster. What do you say? Shall us set up together? He was not really disappointed at my answer. He expected it, but would have liked me to have said 'yes' as he was getting too old to stand up to young blacksmiths like me, and a suitable arrangement would have made his hard life easier.

My life really did not begin until I left England and its people who looked down their noses at a mere blacksmith. Both parents being dead and with all other relatives unknown to me I thought that I could do worse than go to a fresh country where I might be accepted in my own right. It cost me what little I had saved since coming out of my indentures plus my share of the takings to get a passage, and the fact that I was extremely handy with metal working helped me on the ship where I assisted the ship's carpenter. By good fortune he knew Alfred Trimble whom I had met in the past. I had a name or two of persons who might help me in Sydney, which is where I was going. I sought someone there, who bore the same strange name as myself: Pip. I also sought a young woman who knew Pip, Estella, and a Lady, Lady Amanda Jane Spens. All the latter might know where I might find Pip Pirrip.

Chapter 2

In Sydney

Arriving in Sydney, my enquiries led me to a firm of booksellers, where I hoped to find Jane Alambard. Jane had been Lady Amanda Jane's servant. I was surprised at the hostility that I received as I asked after Jane. I was told rather grudgingly that she had married and her husband, having died, she was now a widow called Jane O'Brian. Some of the hostility went when I mentioned that I was also looking for someone called Pip Pirrip. Then, with the arrival of Estella Brown, all further coldness melted away as they heard how I had come from England, looking for my namesake. Olivia scolded her mother at being so difficult, who looked not a bit abashed. Her excuse was that it was wise to hold back until you knew who was asking after you.

I was taken round to Pitt Street by Lizbeth and Olivia where they told Pip's landlady that I was to be given a room until he returned. A very pleasant room it was, except for the constant noise that came from the street outside. During the hot night it persisted so that I could scarcely sleep. I was also troubled by biting insects.

When I told Olivia about this she laughed and said that in time they would cease to bother me, as my blood would change once I had been in New South Wales long enough. I was encouraged by the laugh for, up to now, Olivia had maintained a staid demeanour more fitting for a matron than a young woman. With her pale complexion, bordering upon the bloodless, her smooth cheeks and straight blonde hair pulled back, she stood out against her friends who were so dark by comparison. I was so taken by her china blue eyes that startled me when I first saw them. Every move that she made entranced me. She was quick, determined and deft in every action. Her whole being resembled a china doll, but I found in time, like china, she was hard and even brittle.

By contrast Lizbeth was dark and lively. She was much more friendly and inviting, and I could hardly believe that the two women were sisters. I wondered whether she had a different father, as Lizbeth was so different in looks to Olivia. It was only later that I found that they were not related. I had made a mistake as Lizbeth was more or less treated as one of the family.

I was also pleased to be fed meals that were so much finer than I had had to endure upon the boat. I had quite settled in when Pip arrived back from New Zealand, where he had been dealing with the setting up of a branch of the firm of which he was a partner.

I think I must have shocked him somewhat as, at first, he seemed unable to comprehend who I was. Then he collected his wits and took my hand readily, and a mighty soft hand I found it too in my stout paw. We were all soon sitting at ease, and talking over old times, when John Adam called, causing Estella to jump up and hurry off with him. He had called on previous days, when I had observed similar quick exits. It was very plain to me that both were enamoured with each other, a fact that had been confirmed by Jamie, Olivia's brother. He had spoken quite openly to me about the way in which Pip had gone to New Zealand leaving Estella high and dry. I tried to find more from Olivia and her mother, but both turned down their mouths and changed the topic.

No one moved with more grace than Estella; no one outdid her in charm; no one exceeded her in serenity, but it was all bloodless. She was the remains of the perfect English lady; an English rose just slightly past it's best. She made no effort to be a lady. It came naturally. Her only effort was to attempt to hide any emotion, as any display of anything other than gentle amusement would be seen by her as vulgarity.

Pip seemed surprised to see Estella run off. I started to say something, but stopped as a soft kick under the table from Olivia along with a warning look made me think that I had said enough.

To be honest, I was disappointed when I finally met Pip. At first, when we all sat together, it had been interesting to meet someone of whom I heard my Ma and Pa speak so frequently. My father, in particular, was fascinated by the way that Pip had been plucked from the forge to be transformed into a gentleman. I knew all about Pip's early life, having heard it many times. I also knew all about Magwitch's return. My Pa thought that Magwitch had been stupid; he could easily have sent a letter asking Pip to come to Australia. From what I heard though, Abel Magwitch, though a determined man, was rather simple, some would say naïve, bearing in mind what his life had been.

I had heard the story of how Pip and Herbert Pocket had tried to get Magwitch away by boat, and it always seemed to me that both had been so carried away with the romantic notion of helping an escaped convict that they had neglected the essentials. All that dressing up and hiding in inns! If they had simply gone straight away, they would have accomplished it, and Pip might have been much better off as a result. Now he had to work for a living, no bad thing in its way, but he could have been the gentleman that Abel Magwitch wanted him to be.

I had also heard how Pip had had to be rescued finally by my father, and nursed back to health by my mother. There was also some tale of debts having to be settled that I never really understood. In addition I had a very incomplete understanding of the way in which Pip and Estella parted in England. Now she was here, and again I didn't understand what was going on. What I did understand was that I had to adjust my ideas about them. They were older, of course.

If anyone considered himself as everyone's betters, that person was Pip Pirrip Esq. His beautiful manners, matched only by his elegant dress and perfect bearing, proclaimed how he considered a gentleman should present himself in any situation where he found himself. I expect he thought that he was a cut above all in the goldfields despite having to be rescued by John there several times! I thought he was a prig. Doubtless many took him at the value that he placed upon himself; he certainly put himself in the highest ranks of Sydney society. I wondered how he could bear to bring himself to work.

I was much more impressed by John Adam, who seemed to me to have a much better grasp of the realities of life. He accepted my interest in pugilism, listening with apparent interest to how I had moved from a simple puncher to a more scientific fighter. He also appealed to me as a truly self-made man. I thought that Pip, with all the ways in which he behaved, was by contrast, effete.

From Pip's description of what John was like when they were both in the goldfields, he must have been a dashing, handsome example of manhood. No wonder that he captured the infamous Lola Montez, even if it was only until she took up with another lover. Now however, he was portly and his ruddy cheeks betrayed his devotion to wine, and the other good things of life. He still was an awesome being who could stop conversation and turn heads, male and female, as he entered a room; less nowadays from his physical presence, and more from the simple fact that he was rich and powerful.

Both Estella and Olivia treated me kindly, but distantly. I expected no more from Estella. She was in the middle of what was obviously a trying time when she was letting go of Pip, and taking up with John. It seemed to me that Pip had treated Estella shamefully by ignoring her. Olivia's coolness was another matter. It bothered me, as I had always been able to charm my way with women of all sorts and ages. Mrs O'Brian, for example, was soon much friendlier. She enjoyed an audience and loved to tell me about how she and Lady Spens had managed in their first years in the colony. She made no bones about being transported and being a servant. What interested me about most, however, was her deferring to the gentry as she called them. Why, I wondered did she not share my view of them, considering her history?

Chapter 3

Work in New South Wales

I had left England where the poor are so badly treated by those who live upon their backs that there was no future in England for me. I left in order to find a country where an honest man might find honest employ. I hoped that an honest, hard-working, skilled craftsman might make his way and perhaps his fortune. I was no Dick Whittington, but I was a fully trained blacksmith, having completed my indentures successfully. I could work up almost any sort of wrought iron that could be desired. Give me the pattern, and I would produce the finished article.

I was disappointed. It's true that I was able immediately to earn enough to live a more than reasonable life. I was able to use those skills that gave me such satisfaction in some of the work that I did. I was able to compete with others who would have liked to have been as skilled as I was. But, as usual, they were jealous and spoke to employers behind my back, telling them I was not likely to be able to complete what I set out to do.

It had been the same in England. So many times my work was cut short, as they said that I took too long to complete it. It was then given to others to finish. And, when I inspected their efforts, I found imperfections and mistakes. That was one of the reasons that I turned to prize fighting. After a few jugs of ale I tried myself at a local fair near Canterbury and found that my reach and solid hitting worked well. An old pro took me in hand, saying that I should learn more about the new scientific methods. At first I scoffed at him. He took me to see others fight and I began to apprehend what this might mean. For a while I even attended an establishment that was set up to follow Mendoza's methods. I was turned off eventually as being too erratic. They meant that they thought that I should not drink, but surely everyone drinks?

The other thing that appalled me was the way in which many in New South Wales had become property owners and were now putting themselves alongside those high and mighty folk who came out from England to lord it over ordinary folk. What is it that comes over ordinary men, the minute that they begin to raise themselves? Why do they think that having bettered themselves, and I do admit they have done just that, that that gives them the right to throw their weight about and presume that they are now able to order around those who are less fortunate. Where is their charity?

Chapter 4

More Fighting, and Drinking

On the boat I had several times been forced to defend myself, for there were two men who would otherwise have been ready to take advantage of me. After one such bout, a gentleman told me that he had wagered several guineas upon me, and had been pleased to make money from it. He proposed that proper bouts should be staged and that he would run a book. I was nothing loath. I had been involved in this way many times. What I did not tell this swell however was that many fights were rigged, and these ones could be too.

I looked for my two opponents below decks where it was quiet, and we came to a mutually satisfactory agreement. This involved making sure that we put on a good enough show whilst ensuring a final outcome that made money for my gentleman swell. He was not as green as I took him for, for when he paid me he let slip that he was well aware of the way we had fixed things and hoped that once we had arrived we might do some similar business again.

So when I found myself out of work I sought him out and in between spells of employment I began to establish myself as a pugilist of some standing. Some bouts I genuinely won. Others were rigged, as usual, allowing us fighters to protect ourselves and to have re-matches where we earned more than if we had fought only the once. There is great art in pugilism, some of it is to do with actual fighting, while some of it, sometimes the major part, depends upon acting. Despite all that it's thirsty work and after a fight I would be treated liberally to whatever I wished to drink, and as a consequence I must admit that I was more often than not totally intoxicated. Mind you, it took plenty to get me into that final state; for I was a dedicated toper, always had been, probably always will be.

I tried to keep all my fighting from Pip Pirrip, as I thought he was more interested in my activities as a blacksmith, him having been taken from that trade to be gentleman. When we met I was sure to acquaint him with my success in blacksmith work, and was gratified that he swallowed whatever I told him on that score. It was not so easy to fool Olivia nor her Ma, especially Mrs O'Brian. She had come to where she was the hard way, and knew fraud when she saw it. When I was matched against the Tasmanian Devil and won, I slipped away for I knew that having put him down, I had achieved a certain notoriety.

As time went on and I got less work I tried to get more bouts. At first it was easy enough. I was young and fit and could make a match with any bruiser that they put up. Some were pitiful specimens. They could hit, but with no skills to avoid my blows they would shamble around while I danced close enough to land a series of telling blows, then danced away leaving them to call out:

"Stand still and fight."

I saved my breath. I needed it to make my legs work. Too often they were tired before I was declared the winner. Once, with a lucky blow, I put down a real strong fellow from the countryside, only to have the scare of having him declared dead. Was I relieved when he came to! His heart had stopped for a moment, then restarted. I bought him a drink afterwards when he told me that this had been a lesson to him. He was never going to try this again, but would go back to where he belonged. He said that it might be a God-forsaken hole but he would be alive there.   He wrung my hand earnestly and I thanked whatever saint looked after Pugilists for I swear that had he hit me just the once. I would have gone down as if pole-axed.

Chapter 5

Dancing Attendance

I didn't want to go. It was a ball where men would want to dance with Olivia. She liked dancing and so did her Ma. In the end I said I would, knowing that at least I would be near her, even if I didn't dance with her. John spent the whole time talking with other businessmen, but he did take us all in his carriage so we couldn't complain. An obnoxious young man asked Mrs O'Brian to dance, hoping to ask Olivia next. Fat chance. Her list was full right up. She really came to life on these occasions and said more than once that it was a pity I didn't dance. 'Well I can dance around the ring', was my usual reply.

Across the room I could see John and Pip who were talking animatedly. Pip was almost poking John in the chest, as he seemed to be emphasising his point of view. It did not seem that John shared that viewpoint for he suddenly lashed out and caught Pip's hand. People around them remonstrated with them both and I heard the sound of a glass breaking. Mrs O'Brian asked me what was happening. Like many ladies, as she had grown older she had grown shorter, so she couldn't see. I could see them all, including Estella in one of her famous ball gowns that must have cost more than I could earn in a week. She turned away, obviously embarrassed, and tried to seem unaffected by the commotion.

"Do go over to find out what is happening," said Mrs O'Brian.

I pushed over to where the two men were glaring at one another. As I pushed through the crowd several men objected until they recognised my face. Flooring the Tasmanian Devil had made me quite notorious. Pip turned away and left, which pleased me, as then I only had to deal with John, who had clearly had too much to drink, yet again! His shirt was ruby red with spilt wine. I later found that Pip had actually thrown it over him.

"Time to go, Mr Adam."

He looked at me, was about to say something, then thought better of it as I bunched my fists and gave him a steady look, and nodded to agree.

I went back to Mrs O'Brian and Olivia. I was unhappy to see that several employees of John and Pip's firm were there, watching and listening. There were some sniggers, some low remarks that faded away as I gave them a look. I still heard remarks about lost temper, drink, what a shame, and so on.

I told Mrs O'Brian that Pip had gone off in a huff and that John would wish to go home now as well. He joined us, red face to match a now red shirt. No matter, I thought, he has washerwomen in plenty to deal with that, although I suspected that he would simply throw the shirt away. Despite my black looks in his direction, the obnoxious popinjay who was hoping to dance with Olivia said that he would stay with the ladies while I went to fetch the carriage. John had already intimated that he wanted me to do this so I went to tell our driver to bring the carriage round.

Out in the warm night air, thick with insects, I waited until they had all got into the carriage and driven off. I said

160

that I would join them later as I had some unfinished business to attend to. The Popinjay made the mistake of thinking that I was the servant of the party and tried to give me a coin. My first blow took him in his stomach, and when he doubled up, a sharp tap on his chin completed his lesson not to presume on my good nature. I gave him back his coin.

Chapter 6

Pip's a Hero

They were all full of it. Seemingly Pip, that mild, gentle soul, had become a hero. I suspected, until I heard more, that he had simply been foolhardy. But no, he really had risen to the occasion and would have made Nelson proud. It was all to do with boats and the sea and saving people from drowning. I never did get the full story despite it being in the papers. Actually, that is not quite correct for the papers were full of the doings of a young lass, who had really saved most of the people on the ship. Pip had been on the ship and she had been on the shore. She rode out to save them and Pip helped them get into the water. Leastways, that was as much as I understood about it. It was all in the papers.

Anyway, it didn't really matter how much I understood, in everyone's eyes he was a hero, and that was that. It didn't alter matters for me. I was still mostly out of work, and finding that a dram with the flash coves who were still willing to pay for it led me into trouble. I wanted to marry Olivia. She knew that I did, but like Toby, who also wanted her to be his wife, she ignored us and our desires. Instead she led men on then rejected them. God alone knows what she really wanted. I could never tell. I could say that her behaviour drove me to drink, but that would not be true, not in the slightest.

She wanted to tell me what she had found out about Pip from a young woman who had been on the ship. This creature was giving theatrical performances, can you just imagine, about the whole disaster. What upset Olivia was my complete and utter disregard of any of this. She just could not see that what concerned me was her and me. Whenever I tried to discuss this she shied away like a young horse that has been frightened by a shadow. Well, I was determined to stick to my purpose. My heart was set on Olivia and the hope that through a marriage with her I might break out of this prison of alcohol where I seemed to have handed down to myself a life sentence of drinking. I knew very well where my careless carousing would lead. God knows, I had seen it often enough in others, many of whom had passed on from this sad life to somewhere else.

Chapter 7

Estella Dies

She was a sweet lass. I never minded the airs she gave herself. She really couldn't help herself. It was bred into her. Her wanting Pip instead of John was so clear that you could have reached out and touched it. I never mentioned it, but she knew I knew. Strangely, of all the so-called ladies, including that paragon of all the virtues, Mrs Chisholm, Estella was the only one that I really had time for. I liked Mrs O'Brian too. She was no lady though. Her no-nonsense manner was refreshing, after the cant of most of the other women. Why she couldn't see how her down-to-earth attitude to life was naturally reflected in her daughter I could never work out. Maybe Livvy did then take it to such lengths that it frightened men off. I think though that it was the fact that she knew about things from books, had opinions, and didn't simper all over the place that stopped many a likely lad from persevering with her.

So I was truly sorry when Estella had that accident. She didn't deserve that. No one should die like that. I know that we all have to go sometime, but still.... I suppose that as bigger and better engines are made to go faster and faster it will lead to more deaths. Olivia was strangely affected by it. She never mourned, but raged instead against the doctors. It was all to do with this idea that she had about nursing. In the end she applied to be trained. Her Ma was livid. She didn't want a daughter of hers cleaning up after others. She knew that nursing meant dealing with the really messy bits of life and death. Livvy saw it all through the distorting words what she had read in books. Those words could never really convey the downright awfulness of illness, mutilations and death. They never said very much either about the way the doctors themselves added to people's misery. Some were so caught up with their own ideas that they ignored what common sense would have told them, had they but listened. Her head was turned by what she had heard about Miss Nightingale. In the end it all worked in my favour as I caught her in a weak moment and got a promise from her if she did not get selected.

Apparently, despite nursing being the muckiest job, they were strict about who they chose. I think they knew that most of these women were out to get a husband, and a doctor would be a prime prize in the marriage stakes. That made them cautious; they had to protect those high and mighty doctors.

Chapter 8

Pip Becomes a Real Gentleman

Olivia's Ma was so delighted about something that she couldn't wait for me to sit down when I came back from work before she announced her news. If it had been her she could not have been more pleased.

"He's got it at last. Now he can be a real gentleman, just as Abel wanted him to be."

She poured me a drink. That was unusual, but I suppose that she thought that by doing so would make me stay to hear her out. She pulled up a chair and I did too, holding out my now empty glass for a refill. As she filled it, she began her tale. It was one that I had heard bits of before; who in that household could not have, bearing in mind the effect that Abel Magwitch had had upon them all?

Jane was convinced that any transported convict who worked in New South Wales was bound to have had some effect upon the future of that colony. If he had children, then there would be descendents; whatever he worked at, there would be a result for his labours, buildings; even those who chose to remain offenders would have prisons and so on as a result of that intransigence. But Abel Magwitch, by his actions, had such an effect on people, that many were affected in all sorts of ways. I too came into that category, for I had come to Australia seeking Pip Pirrip who was the gentleman that Abel desired to create.

Jane O'Brian listed for me on her fingers all those who were, or had been subject to the Magwitch Effect as she deemed it. First there was Lady Amanda Jane. Next came Jane herself, then her husband and her two children, Jamie and Olivia. She even averred that Toby and Lizbeth were part of the total.

" I must not forget dear Estella, so cruelly taken from us," she finished.

She sat back, enjoying me being her audience. She leaned forward, her rough face aglow with the intensity of her feelings in order to carry on.

"These convicts have increased the population, produced food, constructed buildings, made roads and railways that have enabled us to push out into previously unexplored areas."

"They have also killed off many of the original inhabitants, or turned them into a parody of what they were before. They have stolen their lands and corrupted their owners and derided their religious beliefs."

"Oh come now. They have none. They are black savages; but, be that as it may, Abel Magwitch was no different in that what he did now has its consequences. He worked the land bequeathed to him by a grateful master what he rescued from those black heathens. He made it fertile. He sent back money to some lawyer who used it to make a gentleman of Mr Pip Pirrip in England.

We all tried, you know, to prevent him from returning to see his young gentleman. We saw what arrant folly it was to do so. But he was so set on it that we all, even Alfred Trimble, the carpenter that he rescued from drowning, I bet you a guinea that you did not know that, tried to turn him away from his folly."

Actually, I did know about the rescue, but I was not planning to spoil an old dear's pleasure, so I said nothing.

"It took some doing, I can tell you, getting him away on a boat, with him pretending to be a Mr Clovis. We did it though. That feeble husband of Amanda Jane never knew a thing. I reckon that had he known he would have tried to stop us. Too frightened of upsetting the authorities he was all his life. Well he got his reward. They made him a Knight, and made my old mistress a lady. Well that bit pleased me anyway.

She drained her glass, refilled it and made no protest when I emptied the bottle into my empty glass.

"Anyway, we were right to try to stop his foolishness, and, although we were right sorry to hear how it all turned out, him dying in prison and all, we never expected his young chap to come here. But come he did, and soon had his feet well under Arthur and Amanda Jane's table. To be honest I thought he was a sponger. He gave every appearance of being one. He lived off them until he went back to England when he went to see your folks. With no income I think he was looking for some way to make his way in the world. I heard that he went to see Estella too, and it's my opinion that he thought a marriage to her would mend his fortunes. Trouble was, she hadn't any. When he got there, the cupboard was bare!"

I went to stand up, more to relieve myself, rather than to stop listening. Jane looked affronted.

"I'll be back. Just got to..."

When I returned there was a fresh bottle on the table.

"Nothing wrong with a drink to celebrate. Now he's got his inheritance."

"Nothing wrong at all."

I poured myself a drink. Over the rim of my glass I saw Olivia come into the room. She sat down quietly.

"What are you telling him, Ma?"

"How at last Pip Pirrip of Adam and Pirrip, is at last a real gentleman, a real gentleman mind, not a jumped up, lately come upstart like some I could mention, but won't. Those lawyers have found the papers what say that despite Abel dying in England, according to the law here in New South Wales, he owns land and money that was earned by Abel and left legally to his protoshay, so there!"

Beckoning to me, Olivia left the room as her Ma leaned back and closed her eyes. As I followed Olivia, Jane caught my arm roughly, pulled me down and whispered to me in her wine-flavoured breath:

"It's the Magwitch Effect", then chuckled.

Outside, Olivia said that I shouldn't get her old mother drunk so that I could get the story from her. I said nothing to that. It was not the first time that we had been at odds. She completed the story. It was John, Pip's partner, who had started off the search. Olivia thought at first that he felt so guilty that he and Pip had been estranged for so long over Estella that he decided to see what could be found. She had since heard from Elaine though, that John had had enough of Pip's inactivity and had thought that if he could find the inheritance he could buy Pip out of the business. So, it seemed everyone knew some of the story, and everyone seemed to see it differently!

Chapter 9

John's Wedding

The argument began with what Olivia wanted me to wear at John's wedding. It was that Italian bitch's fault. She had decreed that her marriage was to be the affair of the year, unforgettable. My oath, I reckon once it was over there were many who would gladly have forgotten it. The dressing up, the spite, the backbiting, the snubbing of good honest folks and the malicious tales told. I said all that once to Olivia's Ma who said that many weddings were like that, really enjoyable!

Never mind that some of the guests were simple, honest, well reasonably honest, people, those out of the top drawer wanted to grind into their faces the fact that their so-called betters had more money to waste than they did. It made me seethe, it really did. It was not as if the gilded upper class had manners and morals to match their money. And that was the truth: in the end it all came down to money. It made me fair sick I can tell you.

Whatever I said made no difference. I reminded Livvy that you can dress a monkey in a jacket, but it's still a monkey. She ignored that. I wanted to wear my Sunday suit. Liv reckoned that I would shame them all as a consequence. She, and all the parcel of women were in a constant ferment of excitement and couldn't understand why the men weren't similarly so. They missed no opportunity to let us all know how disappointed they were with our hangdog looks and generally subdued air.

Naturally, Pip and John intended to outdo peacocks. John was a dab hand at this sort of thing, having a wealth of experience in dressing as a respectable and prosperous businessman. He always said that you had to dress rich to remain rich. Actually, according to Pip, John went too far, with the result that there was a certain vulgarity in his choice of waistcoats. Pip, by contrast, always looked a proper gent, according to all the ladies.

Of the men, only Jamie and his mate, Amos Bulstode, seemed taken with the idea of dressing up and parading around. I suppose it came natural to them as they did it every weekend. I would see them with a gang of girls around them drinking and making merry at drinking places where I wouldn't go. Fair dos, though, Jamie often got me taken on when I really needed work, and would speak up for me when I got into Livvy's bad books. Amos, his mate, was a strange looking cove. He shaved his head to keep cool, and was a head higher than Jamie. Along with full sensuous lips and eyes that had lashes that were almost so feminine that most women would have given half their fortune to own them, he had a truly muscular body. I had seen him stripped once when he was in a bout. He was a savage. Having downed his man, he moved in to beat him senseless, and would have killed him had he not been dragged off by the bystanders.

I had to give in. Of course, men always do in these matters. I enjoyed it eventually, particularly the drink and the food. What strange stuff these Italians eat! The best bit was at the reception when Jamie and I wandered around admiring the way the new house had been built. Jamie and his mate, Amos, had both been employed in the building and were able to point out bits of work that were the results of their handiwork. Later when I wandered off I heard them arguing about something.

Usually the best of chums, they could fall out over the stupidest of things.

Olivia went off dancing leaving all of us to our own company. Eilaine Pomeroy tried to get me to dance and when I refused sat with me on the staircase and, as we drank, kept up a running monologue on all the high and mighty folks as they waltzed past us. This one was a banker who used his client's money to line his pockets; this one was in John's pocket as far as debts were concerned; another was known to more ladies via their bedrooms than their drawing rooms; this doctor 'assisted' ladies who had gone too far and now regretted having done so; and this young woman knew more about male needs than their desire for a good meal, and so on and so forth.

Sickened by the litany of greed, lust and hypocrisy, I said goodbye to Elaine and went to find Olivia. She had her Ma in tears and was berating Jamie and Amos about something. I insisted that we went home. No one would speak to me in the carriage as we drove along. The town was alive with noise from the crowds in the streets and I was amused when some young larrikins ran alongside shouting abuse at us.

Chapter 10

I Marry

I truly believe that my marriage was only accomplished because of James Barnet's Garden Palace that was going to be constructed in the Botanic Gardens. As it was to be ready for the 1879 Sydney international Exhibition they needed lots of men, so, despite my poor reputation, I was taken on. The other thing that told in my favour was the rumour that they were going to use electricity to make sure that the work was completed in time. I got Olivia to get me some books on this subject and made it my business to learn about this new way of lighting. I learned enough to be able to talk about it as if I could actually set it up. Having worked previously in Sydney on exhumations in a graveyard that had to be cleared I also had a reputation for working through whatever transpired. We had to sink lots of shafts to determine whether the remains of bodies could be moved. Many found this objectionable, but it was merely another job to me. My foreman appreciated that, so when I found he was taking on men I reminded him that I had done him some favours relating to brick built vaults and headstones that had to be disposed of discreetly so as not to upset the gentry.

As it happened, the electric lights all came from England, and were installed by men who came with them, so my bluff was not called. I did, however, make it my business to talk with the men who put on such airs as a result of having such knowledge, and found that a deal of what they did was easily learned. They were pleased to show off their knowledge and I stored it away, for I could see that if they could light a place of work all night, they could light up a complete city in due course.

I had a bit of luck when the architect who had designed the building came one day. I must admit that I spoke out of turn in his presence, but he took it well, and instead of me being turned off, he got me a better job where I could use my skills. Olivia was happy to find that I could work regularly, and that I could keep off the drink. I wasn't, of course, but I tried to limit my intake. I gave her my earnings and I heard her tell her Ma that I was on the straight and narrow at last. We lived in a room over the old shop where she continued to help out. I didn't like the arrangement, but it brought us in a little more cash and kept her happy. My main objection was Toby who could not keep his eyes off her. I offered to smash his pale face in if he as much as touched her and I was gratified to see that when I said that his face went even whiter. He didn't need to say anything. I could see that he would do nothing to upset me.

Toby was as much a part of the O'Brian household as Mrs O'Brian. He was a hard worker, I grant you that. His small squat frame was to be seen every day engaged on the little bookshop's business, scurrying here and there, his normally pale face red with exertion. He was one of those unfortunates who go lobster red in the sun, so he avoided it, preferring the shade. His bandy legs could have been inherited from his folks. He never talked about them. He declared that the past was exactly that, past. We avoided each other.

Of course the work came to an end as the exhibition was opened so I had to find something else. I could have found work as a blacksmith, but it would have meant leaving the city to work in the country. It would also have meant taking Olivia away from her Ma who was getting exceedingly frail.

Soon after our marriage we were summoned to see Pip. So, on a hot, humid Sunday morning we rode over to Satis Novis. I went with mixed feelings for I recognised that Pip had welcomed me when I first came to New South Wales, but I deplored the way that he had assumed all the trappings of the gentry. I had come to Australia to escape that sort of life. Now, here we were on our way to visit an Australian gentleman. To be fair, frail as he was, he still made us welcome. He puffed a bit as he climbed the stairs to show us his view. It was grand, and no mistake, and all stolen from the natives, not that that bothered this Australian gentleman. Abel Magwitch would have loved to see him lording it over us, and them.

We got the story again from him of how he and John Adam had set up a successful business from being in the goldfields, how he had been in the Eureka stockade disaster and other bits of history that he thought fit to tell us. No mention though of Estella, nor of Lola Montez, although I know from Olivia's Ma that both men were somehow caught up with her. She had the full story from Estella, who had been in the gold fields too. When I asked what on earth she was doing there I was told that she was there with that Caroline Chisholm.

After a bit, and some wine, which I took several glasses of, despite Olivia's warning glances in my direction, Pip showed us some old pieces of china that he was obviously pleased to be getting rid of for he said that they were his wedding present to Livvy and me. I tried to look grateful as I lifted them down, and damn me if they weren't so heavy I almost dropped the first piece.

This made Pip cry out that I was to take care, as they were valuable pieces what he had given him by some Chinese Johnnie as he had saved his life. I knew what was coming so I took another drink, ignoring Livvy's frown and her Ma's disapproval. If they didn't know that I liked a dram or two, they ought to know by now. I settled down, declined Pip's offer of a cheroot, and made myself comfortable to hear another story of the old times. This time it was all about some place where they were driving the chinks off the diggings on account of the fact they were stealing them from good honest men. Pip didn't quite tell it like that, but I had heard this story from John Adam who said that the miners were incensed by the behaviour of the godless Celestials who worshipped all sorts of idols contrary to what they ought to do. He thought Australia was meant for white people, not black nor yellow.

I must have nodded off, for everyone was looking at me strangely, so I said that it was no wonder that Pip had been rewarded so handsomely. Olivia looked relieved. She told me later that when I came out with that, it looked as if I had merely been resting my eyes, not sleeping. I told her that I saved sleeping for my bed as I got little other activity there. This made her put her lips together, and then say that I need not be so crude.

I put the old china pieces in the carriage, taking care whilst Pip was watching, to handle them as if they were eggshells. At home I waltzed them upstairs and poked them into the attic. I told Olivia that after all that effort I needed a drink. Her look inflamed me, so I took my coat and went out.

And that became the pattern of our lives. With a wife who was that only in name, I looked to other pleasures, and a dram eased many a hurt. If I was working, then I had cash. If I was unemployed I found other ways to get at the cash that was made in the shop. At first I simply took something from the till. Wasn't I married to the owner's daughter? Didn't that give me some rights?

They took to locking the money away, but I could usually wheedle Liz into letting me have some. I told her that it was only a loan and that I would pay it back. She would look doubtfully at me, but a smile from me and my friendly kiss usually led to her letting me have something. The time came though when even that stopped. They must have said something to Liz for she shook her head, no matter how much I sweet-talked her.

That was a pity for I think Lizbeth liked me a lot. She was a really beautiful woman with the darkest of eyes and eyebrows that all the men who came to the shop seemed to find irresistible, despite her obvious dusky skin. She had a straight nose but her curly hair made me think she could not be other than half native. In fact, I more or less knew that this was so, for I remember Livvy's Ma saying that Lizbeth had been brought up by her father's second wife, her mother having died giving birth to Lizbeth in the bush. She spoke perfect English, better, in fact, than my utterances.

Occasionally, when no one was around, I poked about and usually found something that was left around, or put by for some reason, like that money in a bottle hidden away with some old books. I thought as how I might come back for the books so as to sell them, but when I looked later on they were gone. I had a strong suspicion that Toby had taken them. He saw me looking in the place where I had left them. I caught him spying on me out of the corner of my eye. I whirled around but he slipped away like an eel that hasn't taken the hook thoroughly. I said nothing. How could I? I was as guilty as he, for I fully intended to convert them into grog.

Chapter 11

A Killing Blow

The trouble with having a reputation as a fighter was that men who knew that I had put down the Tasmanian Devil and floored Billy Granger wanted to have a go at me. They were usually drunk, or they would not have even considered it, and often egged on by their so called mates, but they were a bloody nuisance. This one, because of his size, thought that he could take me easily. If he had managed to hit me I would have had a hard job to keep standing. But time in the ring and lots of brawls had taught me a thing or two. The first one was to avoid the blow if possible. The next was to parry it. I often caught the arm of a man who was swinging at me and pulled at it so that he was off balance when I struck him, so helping him on his way to the floor.

I sidestepped this man but he turned and caught me a glancing blow that scraped my ear. Then instead of rushing me so that I could dodge and duck, he came at me slowly. I realised two things straight away. He was not drunk nor was he a novice. I let him come to me so he was moving, and therefore more unbalanced than I was on my two feet. His next blow was swifter than I expected it to be, but still I avoided it, and managed to get a stinger to the side of his head. He only managed to hit me once more and for that I put my boot against his shin and ran it down until I finished by standing on his foot. Then as I did so, I hit him in the guts, which made him drop his head towards me. My right fist caught him, but not on his chin as I had planned. Instead he caught the full force of my blow in his throat.

His fall was the most dramatic part of the affair, for up to then it had been no more than a messy brawl. I was dragged away into another room leaving him to lay unconscious. Someone threw some water on him. My back was slapped and I was given drinks that I didn't want, and praise for something that had given me no pleasure. I sat in the corner nursing my hands where I had bruised them. One of them had bled. The other was simply bruised. I licked my knuckles. A table next to me held full glasses of grog given me by those who considered I was their man. While we sat there in a babble of noise and a haze of smoke from cigars and pipes a bucket of dirty water was brought to me. It got hotter and noisier. I rinsed my hands feeling the sting go somewhat from them.

A man pushed his way through the crowd and stumbled against the table almost upsetting it. I steadied it. He dropped to his knees bringing his mouth to my ear. His breath was hot.

"He's dead."

I didn't waste time asking who he was talking about. I stood up to a cheer, pushed the bucket to one side, shook off restraining hands and started moving. The longer I lingered the more likely that I was to be taken up. My well-wishers were now my enemies. Outside I found that I was too late. They were already there, waiting for me in the heat and dark of a Sydney night. Insects hummed. As my eyes got used to the dark I spied two men.

Chapter 12

I Go to Become Abel

"That's him!"

"Who are you?" asked one of them, while the other shone a lamp in my face dazzling me.

Confused, something made me say the first name that came into my head.

"James O'Grady."

"I knew it. A Bloody Mick!"

The light was lowered and I saw behind the police a face that had eyes that slid to the right. I followed them and saw Toby. Just as I did so he beckoned to me. At the very same moment both policemen collapsed in front of me. Toby beckoned more urgently. His lips made 'Run' but because of the noise of the fight that was going on, I couldn't hear him. I walked towards him wondering what he was doing here in the docks.

He seized my arm and pulled me round the corner pressing some money into my hand.

" I said run. You can't stay here. You've killed a man. You'll swing for that."

"He attacked me."

"Others will say otherwise. Go while you can. The police will think that they are chasing James O'Grady, an Irishman. Call yourself something else."

He paused. His eyes shone in the reflected lights off the water in the dock. He smiled.

"Call yourself Magwitch, Abel Magwitch. He's dead. That will confuse them."

He gave a slight laugh. I turned to go. I knew something was wrong, so I turned back. I wanted to ask him what he was doing here. We both heard the approaching footsteps.

"Tell Olivia. Tell Olivia."

"What? What?"

"I'm sorry."

Chapter 13

On the Road

For some while I roamed the countryside North West of Melbourne, thinking that no one would be looking for me there, if anyone was. There were plenty of places that were not big enough for a settled blacksmith and so I picked up occasional work. I found that many a smallholding needed a few little jobs to be done but did not warrant a trip to the nearest town. I avoided places like Mansfield or Beechworth and Glenrowan. I travelled with some iron and some charcoal. Charcoal was produced everywhere, as there was a surfeit of old trees that could be cut down. I did small repairs and even made some tools, mainly farm implements, but shutters needed handles and gates needed fittings. Whatever I did I usually only got a meal and a bed as payment. Sometimes I made a little money, never very much. No one was rich. What a contrast to Sydney where the swells rivalled those in England. And so I saw that even in this country of opportunity the old system of grinding down the poor went on as usual.

They were good to me, never asking too much about my past. Too many had pasts that they wished to move away from. I moved constantly, never really escaping, for in my dreams I still felt my fist sink into that joker's throat. I never meant to kill him. It had never been my intention to do that. It was not my fault that he had died, but what did that matter? They were sure that I was to blame, and in time I came to believe it myself. Why otherwise was I fleeing? In time I came to see that I was not trying to escape my past but to escape from myself.

Some were more welcoming than others. A young woman who had been milking her Pa's cows carried over to me her pail of milk and urged me to dip my tin cup into it. It was thick and creamy and reminded me of England. She would have lingered except that her Ma shouted at her to bring in the milk. Later she brought fresh baked bread, not sourdough, but made with real yeast and still warm from the baking along with some slices of mutton. I wrapped the mutton in the bread, and ignoring her, I ate it grateful that I still had enough teeth to do so. Once again she was called away and I ignored her backward glances as I finished what she had brought and concentrated instead on a small job that I had in hand.

Her Pa came out to watch me and while he did so he said:

"They are at it again."

"Who?"

"The Kellys."

"Who are they?"

He looked at me in astonishment, his mouth agape. Some tobacco juice dribbled down a dirty, unshaved cheek. I could see that at the back of the quid in his mouth he had several rotten teeth, and I resolved to offer to remove them. One thing about my trade, I always carried pincers, and I had used them to good effect having seen such activity in the fairs in England.

"The Kellys. Well the Kellys are really making the traps look foolish, and more luck to them say I, for we didn't come to this land to be chased around by police who are just jumped up scoundrels. We want to be left alone to carry on our lives peacefully."

" So, who are they, these Kellys?"

He spat and cut off some more tobacco to replace what he had spat out. He thought for a moment then said:

"They are heroes."

It took a while for anyone else to tell me more and as I learned about them I realised why they were regarded as heroes. And I realised why it was difficult to learn about them. People who venerated them as fighters against an unjust authority were suspicious of me and my questions. Perhaps I was a spy, trying to trick them into telling where the Kellys were, so that they could be shot. That's right, shot. No one thought that the police would try to capture them for a trial. I suppose that I could see the sense of this, for as I learned more about the way the Kellys had carried out robberies and shootings, it seemed to me that, of course, the police would set out to shoot first if they got lucky, then bring in the ones that were not dead for them to be hanged.

The grandfather of this family had been transported from Ireland and kept in one of the worst prison islands in Australia before being released. With no means of getting back to Ireland he had gone to Melbourne. Then, having married into another Irish family, he was constantly chased by the police who knew for certain sure that, as an ex Irish felon he was not to be trusted. In time, they managed to arrest him and after some time in prison he was released to die. The fact that they were all Irish and Catholic did nothing to help them. 'Dirty Catholics' was the usual term of abuse that they attracted, although, having myself seen the sort of life that people scratching a living from the soil in those parts led, it was clear that they would always have good honest dirt on them.

What caught my interest was the mention of a fight that took place when Ned Kelly fought Wild Wright at Beechworth. This fight was talked of most everywhere where they talked about the Kellys; how Ned, despite being smaller, had beaten Wright into the ground so that he had been unable to come up to the scratch mark.

I did not learn much more about the Kelly family until I came slap up against some of them. There were five in all. They came out of the bush on their horses and rode straight into the clearing where I was working some iron fillets for a nearby farm where they wanted their shutters to close tight in July to keep in the warm, as it could be so cold, even snowy. The settler and his wife told me such tales about chilblains that were their lot when they were young, as they lacked being shod properly. When it came to food or clothes, food always won. That was why they liked to buy flour in sacks, as the sacks could be used as clothing. Now they wanted their farmhouse to be as warm as possible.

Nobody said anything. They simply sat on their horses and looked at me. I carried on working. After a spell they got down and let the horses graze while they sat around the fire. I threw more wood on to it. The one who seemed to me to be the leader, introduced himself as Edward. This produced a snicker from the others. Looking furious with a redder face than the one that the wind had already burned up to a good red colour, he amended it to Ned.

I put out my hand and said whatever name I was using at that time. I changed it from time to time.

"A blacksmith?"

"As you see."

"What can you make?"

"Most any thing, give me enough iron and charcoal."

" Come with us. We have work for you."

"I must finish this."

He took it from me and threw it down. I picked it up and reheated it before putting it upon my small anvil. I worked it some. No one said a word. If anything Ned's face became redder. A young man moved closer to me and raised his hand.

"No!"

Ned's sharp word stopped the blow.

"He's right. He must finish what he's started."

I completed the job, giving it to the man who had asked me to do it, and watched carefully to see what the young farmer thought of my new companions. He didn't seem at all concerned, but bearing in mind that it was me who was being taken away, perhaps that was to be expected. They mounted up. I packed up my things and we were away.

Chapter 14

Making Armour

We crossed several creeks that were all full, feeding down to the Murray that was flooding. The homesteads that we passed were small, mostly miserable places with just here and there an occasional well-maintained place. We skirted most places; the group seemed to want to avoid contact with anybody. I tried to ask what sort of work they had for me. Was it agricultural, some farm machinery?

They all kept silent. The last part of the journey was the most difficult as it was continuously uphill. I had to urge my horse to greater efforts in order to keep going in the track that had stopped being a road long since. Then we arrived at a shack that was as tumbledown as any I had seen. I saw to my horse, letting him go free to graze and making sure that he had water. By the time that I had done this, the others had all dismounted and disappeared.

Ned came out of the shack with a paper in his hand.

"See here mister. You see this picture?"

It was in a newspaper that was old and tattered but readable. The picture was of a ship. I looked at it. It was a Yankee ship and I read below it that it was all covered in iron. I read how in the war they had covered ships to protect them from cannon. It didn't explain how the ships did not sink under the weight of all the iron, nor how the iron was attached. Instead it described how cannon balls bounced off the plates.

They called the iron that was on the ship, plates. I imagined round dinner plate shaped slabs nailed somehow onto the wooden walls much as iron horseshoes are nailed onto horses hooves. I waited as I didn't know what I was expected to say or do. Then he said the one word:

"Armour."

In the old days I knew that they had made suits of armour so I presumed Ned was trying to tell me that he wanted something similar. I knew from what I had learned of the Kellys that as bushrangers the police would be after them and would try to shoot them. He had eluded the police so far as he not only knew the country, but also had the support of the little people who saw him as being on their side. I asked him whether he wanted armour for himself or all of them. He nodded and led me over to the back of the shack where I saw some really rough efforts had been made.

I had to laugh at their feeble efforts. They had the right idea, but no conception of how to make it. Seeing my amusement Ned tried to win my support by offering me money. I told him that I was not interested in any money; I simply wanted to get back at those who I reckoned had served me ill since I came to this accursed country. As a blacksmith I could make exactly what they wanted as long as I had a supply of sheet iron and charcoal. These he promised to get me. I did not have to wait long, for the gang were something of folk heroes, as many of the police were cruel and carried out their duties with a lack of humanity that served the gang well. Many saw them as taking a stand against inhuman authority that they thought they had left behind in Ireland or in England. They showed me old ploughs that they said had been given them by supporters.

The following day we rode over another creek to where, at the edge of a copse, there was a charcoal pile being tended by a young woman. It was immense and must have taken days to burn through for I could see that it was at the end of the process. As we rode over to it another, even younger women, pushed aside some rotten canvas and stood up. She had been asleep whilst the older girl, for I could see now that they were both scarcely more than girls, had tended the pile. The younger girl smiled but the older one looked sullen.

I told them that I needed leather, wood, and a trumpet. This item, the last of my demands made them stare.

"If I am to make anything worthwhile, I need to construct a better set of bellows. It's too difficult for me to make the nozzle so I will destroy a perfectly good trumpet for the piping. Out of that I shall make the parts that I need. I also need two strong men, one to pump the bellows and the other to strike where I indicate thus."

I used my light hammer to hit a piece of metal to show them just what I meant.

" I will use the bellows to get a really, white hot heat in the burning charcoal where, at first I will make rivets. I will rivet the armour together. How many men do you say will need armour?"

Ned pointed at himself and then counted off his fingers.

"There's Joe, Dan, Steve...."

He stopped.

It took many days labour, and during that time, newspapers were brought up to us. They said in some that Ned and the others were simply highwaymen, living on terror. Others made him out to be a hero of the people. All accounts were untrue. They simply told people what they wanted to hear. I have met many men over the years. Most either sided with injustice, or sat quiet under it. Just a few, and Ned was such a one, blazed out at those that he thought were responsible for grinding him and his family down. He couldn't stop himself. Once he was started on his path, he was doomed. I knew that and yet I helped him. Don't ask me why. I cannot tell you.

I do know some of his history, for, as we worked on the armour together, he told it me. How he lost his father, how his mother was betrayed by so many people, how he was inveigled into being a bushranger when he was so young he hardly knew what he was doing. I listened in silence, only breaking it to ask about the time that I heard he fought as a prizefighter. He denied it being a prizefight, but agreed that there had been bets on the other man winning. He told me that he regretted winning in some ways because every young fool wanted to take him on. I knew just what he meant.

"But I heard that you fought for money."

"I did fight once, but not for money. It were under the Marquis of Queensbury rules, they said, but I did it for revenge. I wanted to wipe out an insult. That's the Kelly way."

When we finished the armour, it was tested by one of them firing at it. To my absolute horror this was done by one of the boys wearing it and another one shooting at him. It passed the test, but I knew that the police had much better, more modern rifles that might do greater damage. I tried to tell Ned this. He swept my arguments aside. I could see that he was beyond reason. My time with him had taught me that, although he was not stupid, he could be pig-headed. He told me that my work was done and that I should go away now. I thought that at least I had provided him with some protection so that he could escape capture.

Chapter 15

Capture and Trial

They rode off and I collapsed on a heap of musty rotten sacks. Margaret, called Maggie and Katherine, who answered to Kate, both lay beside me as tired as I was. I had done my best, but I still could not be sure that a modern rifle at point blank range would be stopped by what I had wrought. I had seen the effects of such weapons and knew what they were capable of doing. For a while I slept, being woken by one of the girls who had cooked some bacon and made some tea. We had to drink the tea without milk. Then we slept again.

In time we roused ourselves and followed the others away from the shack. My intention was to go back over towards Wangaratta. I had no idea what Ned intended to do, and I was horrified when it became apparent, days later, that he had taken hostages and was holed up in a building. I had to see what the end of all this was, so I travelled to where this was going on and joined the crowd of onlookers that had gathered there. You would have thought that it was a show that had been specially put on for a holiday the way people squeezed together to see what was happening.

From where I was standing I could see a big building, a hotel beyond some trees. People around me were saying that as soon as the police arrived they would undoubtedly attack. Even as we watched, a man ran from the building towards us.

Everyone pressed back until it became clear that it was not one of the Kellys.

He passed us still running. I turned around to see where he went, I couldn't see him, but in any event it didn't matter as a train drew in at that moment with a host of men on it. I could see that, apart from a contingent of police, there were also others on it.

"Who are they?"

"Reporters."

I walked over. The noise was terrific, people shouting and horses neighing. I wandered totally unchallenged amongst the crowd, as the horses were unloaded. No one seemed to be in charge. It was chaotic. What a rabble.

Finally, someone marshalled the crowd of armed men and led them towards the fence beyond which was the hotel where the Kellys were waiting. I thought that someone would call on the Kellys to surrender. Instead there was a shot, which came from the hotel where, a figure that I recognised, wearing armour that I also recognised, appeared. That shot brought down the man leading the others. Immediately everyone seemed to fire at once. The noise was terrific.

The figure in the armour called out something, but, it was muffled by the helmet so we could not make out rightly what he shouted. Bullets thudded into his armour. A shot struck him in the leg. He staggered. Another shot hit him, this time hitting his foot. He staggered again and went back as a dozen men at least shot at him. We heard screaming; either a girl or child had been hit.

Then I saw a sight that I thought I never would. It was Ned riding away and deserting his mates. I ran towards him. He turned, and as he did so fell heavily from his horse. Before I could reach him he had regained his feet and returned, limping to the veranda.

Knowing that he was wearing armour that would not stand up to continual fire I walked away. Ned was doomed. Why had he taken this step of confronting the Police in this way? I never found out. Even when I read all the newspaper reports later it was no clearer to me. I thought that I was assisting him to remain at liberty. My work was directed at keeping him free, not helping him to put himself into danger.

I went back to my horse, got on it and we plodded back to my cart. Putting the horse into the shafts, I took my place on a pile of old sacks, and slowly drew away. Maybe it was time to return to Sydney. I had grown a beard and looked every inch a country yokel, nothing like the city labourer that I had been. I would go to see if I could pass myself off in a crowd and find what had happened to Olivia.

Chapter 16

Back to Sydney

The city had changed. Its noise unsettled me after the quiet peace of the countryside. Everyone spoke so loudly and moved so quickly. I found my way but marvelled at how many new buildings were under construction. I attracted no interest whatsoever. People just ignored me, pushing me to one side. I still decided, however, that it might be dangerous to be too open so I husbanded my little store of money, garnered over the time that I had been away, by looking for modest accommodation. I had increased it slightly by selling my horse and cart and equipment, figuring that if I managed to get work in Sydney I would no longer need them. There was no shortage of rooms to rent provided I was not too fussy. Several 'ladies' made it clear that more was on offer than a room. I avoided these. My life had been complicated enough.

Knowing that Livvy liked the theatre I took to hanging about where I knew she was likely to go, and sure enough one night I spied her with another woman. They were arm in arm, strolling along in the warmth of the evening after the performance. I turned away, but I think she saw me. They stopped strolling and hurried along and I followed wanting to catch Livvy by herself. They stuck together, and I thought as how I recognised the other woman. I couldn't call her name to mind, but I knew her, I was certain sure.

Feeling sure that I could trust them both, I made up my mind to catch up with them and speak to Livvy. I was drawing close, when damn me! someone else came out of an alley ahead of me and followed them. It was quite clear that he was in pursuit, so I dropped back, pulled my hat low over my eyes and waited to see what would happen.

Although his back was towards me, I could tell that it was Toby. I had seen that back too many times as he toiled in the shop, moving stock, climbing up to put away books, to be wrong. My first thought was to run after him, grab him and confront him. I stopped. I thought. What if he was concerned for his employer's daughter's safety? What if he was supposed to keep a covert watch to that end? I had been away. Maybe things had changed more than just new buildings. I resolved to give him some leeway, to allow him to demonstrate his allegiance, if in fact, that was what it was.

The two women took a cab and so did their pursuer. I took the next one off the rank and we all trotted along. They went to a part of the city not known to me, alighted, and entered a house. When the first cab had gone, Toby, for I saw now quite clearly that it was indeed he, loitered outside. I had my cabbie go past and round the corner where I paid him off. He trotted away as I slowly I eased myself around the corner in a shady spot where a tree stood. There stood Toby. Why, I asked myself?

A woman came out of the house and Toby pressed himself back so that she passed him without seeing him. The woman seemed to be the same one that had accompanied Livvy. I was not absolutely sure for I was watching Toby who, when she had gone, took a key from his pocket and used it to open the door and go inside.

I went towards the door and had my hand upon the doorknob. Behind spoke a woman in a voice that I recognised.

"It is you, isn't it?

I turned to see Lizbeth. I took off my hat. She smiled in recognition. She looked older. I suppose that I did too.

"Where have you been? I knew Olivia had seen someone that she knew when we came out of the theatre. I had no idea that it was you."

"Toby went in here. He had a key."

Her smile went.

"He's no right to have it or to be here."

She took a key from her reticule.

"When Olivia and Mrs O'Brian sold the shop to Toby they moved here. He swindled them, you know. He's a snake."

We heard voices and a crash inside the house.

Chapter 17

Don't be a Fool, Toby

Lizbeth opened the door and, knowing the house, led the way along a small corridor into an equally small room furnished as a sitting room. There stood Toby with a knife in his hand sweating and across the room was Olivia, holding her hands up before her as if to defend herself. I told Toby to drop the knife. He did so and I hit him. Something gave way within me as I did so, but I kept enough control of myself not to do more than floor him for I knew that if I did hit him again I might kill him.

We revived him with water thrown over him from an ewer. Now, I said, we shall all sit down together and hear the truth. Olivia sent Lizbeth to make sure that the front door was locked and bolted, then asked Toby why he had come in with a knife, and where did he get a key?

After a pause, Toby then shocked us all with his tale of how he thought he had been so badly treated that he had to have revenge. It all came out, his jealousy of me, his plot to get me to run away, his scheming to take over the shop and how he had watched for an opportunity to come in when Lizbeth had gone and Mrs. O'Brian was drugged.

I looked hard at Livvy when I heard that last part. She made an impatient gesture and said that I didn't know what trials they all had all been put to. I suppose we thought that with the front door shut, we had Toby safe. We were therefore taken totally by surprise when he suddenly sprang up and violently threw us against one another. The room being so small we were unable to move freely enough to apprehend him.

He burst through the door and we heard his boots on the stairs. Scrabbling after him I saw him getting out of a window. He stood for a moment on the windowsill reaching above him. He pulled himself up and we heard him on the roof.

I climbed too and followed his example of drawing myself up by clutching the gutter. It was only by pressing my boot against the side of the window that I managed enough pressure to enable me to pull myself onto the roof. God alone knows how he had managed to raise himself over the gutter. Although it was dark I soon spotted a darker figure outlined against the sky.

"Don't be a fool, Toby."

His answer was to throw himself at me. I only survived as I was clutching the chimney pot. He clawed at my throat. I hit him and he went limp. Now inert, he slowly began to slide down the roof. I grasped his collar but his weight was too much for me. I felt myself being dragged down with him. I had to let him go. He slid to the edge of the roof and miraculously stopped. Taking off my belt, I hooked the buckle over the rim of the chimney pot and holding the end I cautiously edged my way down.

"Get away."

He had come to. The effect of my blow had worn off. My outstretched hand brushed his coat pocket. I tried to grasp it. Just as I had it firm, with my fingers hooked inside, he waved his hand at me as if to say 'goodbye', then with a tearing of the material he finally plunged down as Livvy and Lizbeth screamed together.

By the time that we reached him it was obvious that he was dying. No man could withstand a fall from that height. Apart from smashed legs, his internal organs would have been severely damaged just like that chap who fell when we were building the Garden Palace. We stood around as neighbours came in, attracted by all the noise. Livvy pulled me out of the light and told me to go. She was right. With my reputation, it was better for me not to be on the scene when the police came. So far, no one had commented on my presence, everyone being too busy to see what was happening to the man who had fallen from the roof.

Pulling my hat down I walked away, not quickly, but just slowly enough to give the impression that I had looked in the yard then walked away. My heart hammered in my chest. My hands hurt. I turned back to tell Livvy where I was lodging. I gasped out the address, turned round and continued my flight.

I stayed in Sydney because there was so much work going on everywhere, as everybody seemed to need houses. Other buildings were going up too. I changed my name, kept away from where Livvy told me she was working and found that I was never at a loss for employment. I even managed to get taken on at places where James Barnet was the architect. I had admired him ever since I had met him, when I was taken on to help build the Garden Palace.

There were some who claimed that, later on, when it burned down, it was set on fire deliberately. They pointed to the fact that when the fire destroyed the building, it also destroyed all the native things within it. Removing these, removed the evidence that the aborigines were actually quite intelligent. Whatever the reason for the conflagration, it was a complete disaster, an utter tragedy in the eyes of those who considered that such destruction of the natives' past removed any possibility of understanding them and their culture. I had to laugh at such a word. When you saw the bits of wood and bark and other objects, they hardly stood comparison with what we produced. Granted, they were often colourful, and bearing in mind the primitive tools they had, quite clever but they were no loss to my way of thinking.

I knew that the building had been made of wood, having been associated with its construction, so it was no surprise to me when I heard that it was burning. I hurried over to see it. What a bonfire! They did save some things though. It was a mercy that it happened at night. Almost before the ashes were cold more rumours flew about; one was that the authorities had stipulated a wooden framework so that they could remove the building more easily when it had outgrown its usefulness. Another was that the architect, James Barnet, had wanted a metal frame and brick and glass, but had been overruled on cost. I had admired his other buildings ever since I met him, largely because of the man himself, for I knew that he had risen by his own efforts. As we watched the last part of the building falling into ashes I remembered the time when we had met.

I had been working as a labourer on a lower section of the Garden Palace along with several others, when he had come round with some other men, all flourishing plans and full of their own importance. Not one was dressed other than in fancy suits and top hats. He was obviously in charge by the way the others deferred to him.

"Who's that?"

"That's James Barnet. He planned the building. He's a Government architect."

"Another member of the class that oppresses the poor bloody workers just because of who they know, I suppose."

I had spoken too loudly. James flushed, stopped and walked towards me. My workmates silently removed themselves. They knew my reputation for speaking my mind. They may have been my mates, but they wanted to keep their jobs. He waved away the other two men who followed him.

"Go and check the cross-bracing on the dome."

He stopped in front of me.

"Who are you?"

"Phillip Gargery, a blacksmith, forced by circumstances to work on more menial tasks than I would wish."

" So you have completed your apprenticeship?"

"Yes, and have worked as a journeyman, so I know my trade as well as any man here.

"So we are alike, I suppose?"

"How so?"

"Let me suppose the following: like me, you had parents who made sure that you were raised to a trade; again like me, you worked to improve yourself; you then came, as I did, to New South Wales where you are seeking to make something of your life. Would you not agree that we have something in common?"

"I would readily agree except that you also know people of influence, and that must be of great assistance to you."

"You are right. But mark this Phillip Gargery. You know me now. And what is more to the point, I know you. Go to the foreman and give him this note."

He took a small pocket book from inside his coat and taking a silver pencil he wrote something in it. He took out a page, folded it and gave it to me, then, turning on his heel after nodding to me, he strode off.

His note simply said:

Give this man employment more suitable to his accomplishments.

James Barnet

For a while, I had a much better job. When the building was finished, everyone was turned off. I could have sought help from my benefactor, but something made me obstinate. In fact, there was work a'plenty for those who were sober enough to turn up for it.

The end

Part three

The Magwitch Effect

Olivia's Story

Always a convict's daughter

Chapter 1

Beginnings

When my father, James O'Brian, died I was told that he had had a fever. In no time at all the funeral was held and he passed out of my life. Jamie later on told me that there was something mysterious about Pa's death. I asked him to tell me, but in that maddeningly male way he had, he refused. I think now he didn't really know any more than me.

We went to see Amanda Jane at the farm. It used to be out in the country but now houses were beginning to be built all around. Despite that, they still had pigs and calves and chooks. I always liked the animals more than people. When Jamie and I came in, hoping for some lemonade, or other cool drink that we were often given on the farm, we found Mama and Amanda looking odd. Amanda was holding a watch and wiping her eyes. Mama held us tightly, so tightly that I had to ask her to stop. She cried, but wouldn't say why. She had already cried a lot when Pa died so it was something more. Another grown-up mystery for we children.

Looking back, I suppose that Pa's death was the first thing that I can really recollect, apart from that time when he and I saw the lamb die. I said that I thought it was a cruel thing to happen. He tried to explain that everything has to die eventually. I do have other fuzzy memories, but I know now that some of what I thought I remembered was what Jamie or Ma told me. Ma was a great one for stories, always about the days when she first came to New South Wales. When I was little I listened without understanding, that she had been transported and what that meant. Later on I grew a little ashamed of her origins and wanted her to keep quiet about them. Then, as I grew up, really grew up in my mind as well as my body, I realised just how honest and true my mother was. I determined to be like her. Strangely, her face never bothered me. To me, it had always been rather battered, and I accepted it without question. It bothered Jamie, my brother. I did say once to him that there were many worse things than a battered face; he wanted to know what I had in mind. I reminded him of the Brenville's aunt who had gone mad and had to be put away. That made him thoughtful.

Along with Jamie were Lizbeth Wright and Toby Davis who used to work in our shop. When I was young I thought that they were part of our family. Gradually I learned that they were employed by Ma, but up to the time that Lizbeth left us to get married, they were pretty well treated as family. Toby liked me. Later on I had to turn him down as a suitor, after which things changed considerably, but I am getting ahead of myself.

I cannot recall a time when I couldn't read and write. I was surrounded by books, and I suppose Ma must have instructed me, unlike Jamie who was sent to school. I was fiercely envious of him. Why was he favoured in this way? I longed to know more. He, by contrast, didn't want book learning. He was so clever with his hands. He made me wooden toys, including a cart that really rolled along. I truly loved my brother, and although I was envious of the opportunities for education that were given to him, I was never jealous of him. In fact as I began to realise the special place that women occupied in the world, I rather pitied him. He told me once that the other boys at school laughed at him, as he did not want to join in their rough games. He said that he constantly felt an outsider, and being the son of an ex-soldier who was now a shopkeeper didn't help.

Even as a small boy Jamie was very particular about his appearance, taking extreme care with his hair and getting upset if he got his clothes soiled in any fashion. Not over large in stature, but wiry with a tough frame, he had enormous strength in his fingers. I have seen him pull iron nails out of wood with his bare hands when he was woodworking.

I was told that one day I would be married, then, domestic duties would take up my time. I could already cook, and make bread. I also helped in all sorts of activities like sewing and laundry, so knew what awaited me. Reading books let me escape temporarily, but never for long. I never minded assisting with the chores. Lizbeth and I worked together and we were merry most of the time, despite the hard work. She told me that she meant to marry a lord, no common workman for her. All she wanted was a lord as a husband, and some servants to do her bidding. We both knew that these were dreams.

My position in this women's world was cemented firmly into place one day when Ma told me to put on my bonnet and darkest shawl and go with her. I knew all about childbirth. You could scarcely not know about such matters, as we regularly went into the country seeing rams and bulls and knowing what their place in farms was. I thought that I was going with her to assist in a birth, although she never actually said so.

It was the bag that she took that made me think that I was to be an assistant midwife. She gave it to me and, laden with it we hurried through dirty back streets to a filthy house where I thought at first that we were to be turned away. Inside, I duly handed over the bag, and went to fetch hot water. That took a little while, so when I got back it was pretty well all over. But not so far that I didn't see the end of it and realised that it was not a birth. Now I assisted in cleaning up the young frightened girl who was sobbing quietly. I held her hands and stroked back her damp hair. Ma gave her something to drink, I think it was laudanum, and she soon became drowsy. I had to unclasp her hands from mine as we left and, to be honest, her clutching at me then did more to unsettle me than anything up to that moment. She was so young and helpless.

On our way back Ma told me that I was never to tell anyone about what I had seen. That was the first time that I went with her, and I was to go on similar errands for a number of years. When Louisa Ford was taken up, I persuaded Ma to give it up. I didn't her or myself to be taken to court as she was and be humiliated like that. There were too many people now who saw only one side of this business, and were ready to smash anyone caught in it.

During my reading, I had covered most of Shakespeare's plays but had never seen one on the stage. I loved the way that they were written. It didn't bother me at all that I hardly knew what they were about. I read other books for that. Shakespeare for me was the pure enjoyment of the words. But what a revelation when eventually I heard them spoken by actors and actresses.

Chapter 2

Mr Phillip Gargery

He was a well-built fellow, dressed quietly, but in clothes that were more suitable for a working man. His face was battered and I wondered what such a man wanted in our bookshop, but, apart from that, I took little notice of him. We had men frequently in the shop. Many came to chat with Lizbeth, pretending to wish to buy something in order to gain some time with her. She was clever at dealing with them. They were all made to think that she thought that they were someone special. She did it with looks and her tone of voice. Few went away without buying something. I used to laugh with her after we shut the shop each day as we recalled the various swains who she had dealt with. I used to remind her about the lord that she wanted to marry.

"Did one come in today?"

"Not yet, but just you wait!"

This one was certainly no lord. He had a small piece of paper in his hand and I thought that it might be a book title. He asked for Jane Abelard. I told him that we had no such person here. I added that my mother had been Jane Alambard, but was now Jane O'Brian. At that very moment she came into the shop from the back, where she used to hear most of what went on, and asked if she could be of any assistance.

"I'm seeking Jane Abelard or Alambard."

"That will be me. I was an Alambard, but now I'm Jane O'Brian.

"In that case, do you know a Mr Pip Pirrip?

Mama smoothed down her apron and shot me a warning look. She said nothing. I recognised the signs: she was doubtful about something. Taking my cue I smiled and said nothing.

" My Ma and Pa knew him in England. My name is Phillip Gargery. Alfred Trimble said that I might find him through you."

My mother's attitude changed immediately. She called to Toby to assist Lizbeth and led the young man into the back where she said that she did indeed know a Mr Pirrip. Phillip Gargery, as we found him to be, was a rough-hewn sort of chap. His face was the result of his being a pugilist, a term that I had to explain to all as we sat round listening to how he came to New South Wales. By this time, we had shut the shop for the weekend. We could have sat there forever and a day as he brought us news of England, a country that had transported my mother, and which none of us others had ever seen. It was strange how the mother country exerted such a spell over us.

In time it was decided that we should take him round to Pip's lodging's. In effect it was a set of rooms that he occupied with a housekeeper to look after him. She was doubtful whether she should let him in, but Estella brushed all her concerns aside, saying that as soon as Mr Pirrip was returned from New Zealand he would confirm what she, Miss Brown, had decided. I sensed that Mr Gargery was quite taken with Estella, despite what he later described to me as her uppity ways. He said condescendingly that these were the unfortunate results of her upbringing. Leopards can't change their spots.

Recently I found an old journal of mine where I had recorded the following:

Too conceited for my tastes. I must own though that upon reflection he has a certain manly aire that Lizbeth has also remarked upon, so I could be interested in him. I am prepared therefore for his sake to assist him to better himself, despite his tendency to imbibe strong liquors.

We were all there together when Pip did return at last from jaunting about New Zealand. For about an hour both Phillip Gargery and Pip Pirrip talked about old times. I wondered that Pip Pirrip chose to do so when he had been abroad so long. Surely he would wish to spend some time with the woman who promised herself to him? She sat quietly engaged in some needlework until John Adam called. Up she jumps setting aside her cloth and needle. In no time she had put on her bonnet, the one with the trimmings that I had given her, and with sparkling eyes and pink cheeks she went out arm in arm with John.

Pip stood up and stood as one struck by, I know not what, as they whirled out into the darkness. For a moment we all said nothing. Phillip Gargery opened his mouth but a look from me made him shut it again. The birds outside were still calling in that harsh croak of theirs. I knew, of course, that Estella had planned this stratagem deliberately. My understanding was that she was going to force Pip to declare himself openly and so eventually make sure that he wed her. I say that that was my understanding of the situation. Maybe that was exactly what Estella planned to do. In the event things turned out otherwise.

Chapter 3

Miss Estella Brown

We were on our way to work with the latest arrivals from England, whom I knew would be in a state of some dismay, their hopes and expectations having been raised on the trip, and then dashed upon their arrival in this savage country. Despite a journey where they would have endured the most primitive conditions, they would have imagined that their situation would immediately improve as they set foot upon the shore. It would not have. The plain truth was that even those from the humblest backgrounds would find that they were probably better than the ones that awaited them initially.

My job was to reassure them that this was only the beginning of what could be a most satisfying and fulfilling life. I was supposed to be the exemplar. In me they were to see what one could be with hard work, patience and fortitude. I was not to preach, but to set an example. I also dealt with the hundred and one little matters that were too petty for Mrs Chisholm to have to deal with as she was almost always engaged in a series of skirmishes with higher authority in the Government. This she did to perfection, having learned her trade over a number of years with many and various officials, most of whom seemed to consider it their business to say, 'no' to any positive suggestions.

Despite Mrs Chisholm's efforts to ensure that all these young women were of impeccable character, I was to find each time that not a few were lacking in those womanly traits that ought to distinguish them from men. Some were indeed so lacking in true modesty that it was hard to deter them from throwing themselves at the very first man that seemed in the least part available. In vain, both Estella and Mrs Chisholm urged them to be careful, to wait, to be more feminine and docile. Some, one truly wondered at their upbringing, were like the ravening sea shark or as the prowling tigress seeking her prey.

Others who we were assisting had so many tales to tell about the way men had been instrumental in ruining their lives that either saddened me or maddened me, that I resolved at this time never to trust men again. I knew that there must be some who were noble, kind and thoughtful. John Adam came to mind here. But my experiences in assisting Ma helping young women who had been betrayed in the worst way imaginable by men had made me begin to treat them all with caution.

I talked to Estella about this and her counsel was to remain calm and not to give way to anger or to sadness. She warned me that such excessive emotion would hinder any attempt on my part to assist our poor sisters.

"They look to us to lead them in this new, and to them sometimes frightening, land where we feel at ease. I have come here, as you know, to seek a particular gentleman who I thought had made such a success of his life, despite his humble origins, which I might say I am happy to overlook. I thought that I would be proud to know him, and, should he feel so inclined, to share that life with him. My own past was such that I had to leave England. Although to many I am a lady, inside I know that I am eternally stained by the actions of my mother. I came to start again, just as they do. Let us not be hasty in anything that we do."

I began to say that as the daughter of a convicted felon I hardly felt that I was a good example. Estella stopped me with an imperious gesture.

"You, you Olivia, are precisely the person to whom they should look. Your experience and the way in which you and your family have risen above it, means that they can trust you to understand them. I, by complete contrast, whilst being apparently a lady, earn their respect, but no real trust. They see me as part of that class which they seek to escape. I hope to God that in time we shall have no such class divisions in this new free country.

"Escape? You make it sound as if they are prisoners attempting to escape. Surely, they are all free?"

"Are they? Are we? Are not we all seeking to escape from our pasts?"

As we made our way through the busy streets of what was now a substantial town, Pip hailed us. And I saw Estella grow pale. I asked her whether I should stay with her for she seemed to be so very discomfited. She merely used her parasol to prevent Pip from seeing her lips as she thanked me, but said that I should go on without her. I was doubtful for I knew that, since coming back from New Zealand, he had been active in trying to gain an opportunity to speak to her, and she had been equally active in avoiding him.

It is not my habit to gossip, but if some information comes my way I certainly do not close my ears to it. Thus, I knew that Pip had most shamefully used Estella, leading her on to believe that he wished her to be his wife. His swift departure to New Zealand on the firm's business when gold

227

was discovered in that country spoke most eloquently of his haste to be rid of his promises. To add to Estella's distress, which I must stress she never once mentioned to me, he neglected ever to correspond with her, despite frequent letters sent to John Adam on matters of business.

In all this, John acted with the utmost propriety, seeking to support her in the most gentlemanly way that one could imagine. In my heart, I was sure that, although he wished nothing more than Estella's best interests, he too would have proposed to her had it been at all seemly so to do. When Pip did return, it was to find that his shameful neglect of someone who had been willing to share his life, had laid the foundations of her turning to another.

I reached the shelter where I was soon immersed within a fresh group of young women, and coping with the usual humdrum set of petty matters that I seemed destined forever to be saddled with. A step that I recognised, along with another, that betokened a man, brought both Estella and Pip into my view. My group of geese became animated and several saw no reason why they should not attempt to attract his attention. I made a mental note of the worst offenders. There were murmurs of discontent as both Pip and Estella went into a side room. I hushed my group, set them to sew and went to take tea into the side room.

There, I found them sitting opposite each other, both looking extremely hostile. I can only imagine what subsequently transpired, for Estella, ever the perfect lady, never revealed a word to me. On the other hand, Pip, through his actions told me everything. He burst from the room, clutched his hat before ramming it on his head, and left the shelter as if the devil himself was after him. Then, a few paces from the door, where I am not ashamed to say I lurked in order to see him, he slumped against the wall covering the side of his suit in whitewash. His eyes were bright with tears. They ran unchecked down his cheeks as he sobbed:

"No, no, I cannot. It has to be."

Chapter 4

Rescue

Having warned Ma about the dangers of continuing with her illegal acts, I was appalled to find her leaving the house with the usual bag. I tried to take it from her saying that she should remember the fate of Louisa Ford. She had been caught red-handed, and was even now serving out a sentence in the women's prison. Ma said that it would not happen to her. Someone had informed on poor Louisa. They had been waiting for her. It had been a trap. How ironic it was that this country, built upon the work of convicted felons, should create more convicts out of compassionate women who simply wished to help their less fortunate sisters who had suffered at the hands of men.

I was on edge from the moment that she left. Both Toby and Lizbeth felt the rough edge of my tongue as I found fault in whatever task they set their hand. I was in the shop, glaring balefully at Toby's latest efforts to display our recent stock, when the boy ran in. He could scarcely gasp out his message from his sister, Effie, who had bade him run his fastest to find a Miss O'Brian. His sister was a housemaid and knew me, and knew that I would understand the message that the boy had been carefully coached to say. He was to say that Mrs O'Brian needed a carriage immediately to bring her safely home. He added that he was to repeat the word "immediately", and give me the piece of paper that he had clutched in his dirty hand. It was an address. I looked at Toby, all thoughts of censure of his behaviour now gone. He took off his rough work apron, put on his jacket and put his hat on.

"I know what to do."

Later I learned that he had gone straight to John Adam and had insisted on seeing him. John had immediately, not only put a carriage at his disposal, but had instructed one of his burly retainers to go with it to the address on the paper. He had said to Toby that he was to return to me. He was not to concern himself further with this matter. It was now out of his hands.

At last a carriage drew up at our shop and I hurried to help the driver hand down Ma who had a piece of calico bound around her hand. She smiled shakily at me as I led her indoors. There, I read her such a lecture, once she had taken a small measure of our best brandy, that I almost frightened myself. Then I went upstairs and cried on my bed.

Chapter 5

John Adam

Toby had gone to John Adam, the business partner of Pip Pirrip. John was a most successful businessman, the son of a tailor in Melbourne. Having made his fortune in the goldfields along with Pip, they established the renowned firm of Adam and Pirrip. Whatever John set his hand to in the way of business, it prospered. As Australia burgeoned and expanded and grew rich, so did John Adam. And in so doing he carried Pip along with him. It's true that he was infinitely less a gentleman than Pip, but he had an animal vitality and an acute but crude sense of any situation where money might be made. People said that he exploited others to his advantage. He never denied this. He said that by so doing he made work and riches for many others, and was that so bad?

If only his judgement in respect of ladies, or should I say women, matched his business judgment. The Lola Montez affair, that all seemed to be aware of, was not an isolated incident. There were many others. Successful as he was, he naturally attracted women who hoped to ensnare a rich husband. At least he avoided a disastrous marriage. Well, he did most of his life.

John had more or less rescued Pip when he was at a very low ebb in the goldfields outside Melbourne. He wanted Pip, who he thought was a real gentleman, to put a gloss onto their work. He thought that he could open doors that would be shut to a son of a mere tailor. Pip did his best. He managed to interest John in some of the finer things in life, like Shakespeare. John's taste in clothes however, stayed hopelessly at the garish end of the fashion spectrum, much to Pip's despair.

John loved what he called the good things of life, and being rich, never stinted himself. He was equally liberal in his treatment of his friends, and we were often the recipients of his bounty. He kept a carriage and pair, attended theatres and other social events, ate and drank much more than was good for him, and we, to a certain extent, shared in all this.

If Toby, or Tobias to give him his proper name, had gone to Badger instead of John I should not have been surprised for I knew that somehow he was involved with Ma. This latest episode gave me an opportunity to quiz her about him. Up to now all she had ever said when I had asked her about him was that he and my father had been soldiers together. But when I asked why she was still friendly with him I always got evasive replies.

Now under my relentless verbal assault she gave way. Badger had assisted both Ma and Pa when they had both been threatened by a convict. He had threatened to burn down the shop, and Badger had made sure that he had not been able to carry out his threat. My Ma entreated me to ask no more, but I could not resist asking why he was called Badger.

This provoked nervous laughter. I waited, and then Ma said that I was not to tell a soul but this nickname was on account of his hairy appearance. When he first joined the ranks he enlisted as Eustace Brill which, as Eustace was ever his proper Christian name, he had to have put on the

Regimental rolls. Just imagine how the other recruits used to rag him, calling him Useless Eustace. So when he climbed the ranks for the first time and was going grey he was called Badger. The name stuck. When he was broken down from sergeant on account of some fracas over some missing equipment he left the army, but had to enlist again, as he plainly knew no other trade than bearing arms. This time he swore that his name was Badger Brill and the recruiting sergeant enlisted him under that name.

Chapter 6

At the Theatre

I don't think there was one person in Sydney who had not heard of the infamous, the scandalous, the fabulous Lola Montez once she had arrived in the city. A clever woman, who used her scandals to her advantage, she made sure that everyone knew that she was coming by getting the newspapers to print the following:

"We beg to inform our readers and the public generally that on June 6 the celebrated Lola Montez left San Francisco, at the head of a theatrical troupe of exceptional talent, bound for distant Australia. The public in the Antipodes may confidently look forward to a rare treat."

Ma had read this and as a result wanted desperately to see this lady. It wasn't just that notice that was in all the papers that intrigued her. They also had accounts of all kinds of scandals attached to her name. How pleasant it is to enjoy the virtuous feelings that are engendered by condemning such behaviour, whilst at the same time equally enjoying the frissons of excitement that came from reading about, and discussing in the fullest possible detail every possible aspect of it.

I thought that she must be a clever woman, and I also supposed that she had talent, for she had appeared in numerous plays, including some by Shakespeare. When I said this both Ma and Mrs Leckie laughed. I knew that Ma and Mrs Leckie had been transported and in the process they must have seen, and been exposed to corruption of all sorts and to, I know not what, degree. So it was only to be expected that they would tend to see the worst part of Lola Montez's behaviour as her defining aspect.

Sipping tea together in our back room, we perused those newspapers that Ma had frugally saved, once others had bought and discarded them. Ma had no difficulty in reading them, but as she knew that the Leckies had fewer abilities in that direction, she called on me to read pieces from them aloud. Mr Leckie was nearly illiterate, despite being a successful businessman of a particular sort. An opportunist by nature, he specialised in picking up anything that didn't appear to belong to anyone. Jamie, who knew him, said that he was very like our government in that way. Phillip Gargery was only too ready to agree with that opinion.

So I read these sorts of extracts:

Lola Montez is a comely woman with beautiful eyes; an attractive smile and her crowning glory would be the envy of any woman. However, this actress seems to believe that her performance is enhanced by exposing those parts of her female anatomy which decency would demand should be shrouded. We refer, of course to her legs. We are forced to say this in order to turn young, susceptible men away from her performance where we strongly believe they would be corrupted by such indecent exposure.

Whilst Lola Montez might claim to be a lady by birth, and her calling herself Madame Lola Montez, Countess of Landsfeld is the proof of the claim, if not the proof that she is indeed a Countess, her conduct upon the stage is anything but ladylike. Her constant drawing attention to her lower limbs by raising her skirts enabling the whole world to see, not only her ankles, but also those parts of her female anatomy that it would not be fit to mention in a newspaper, is not the action of a lady. We have few countesses in New South Wales, but we are sure that any that we do have do not behave in this scandalous and libidinous fashion.

When Lola Montez appears in her now notorious Spider Dance, based, she claims, on the traditional Spanish dance, 'La Tarantula', she raises her skirts so high during the dance, that the audience, to their utter scandal and amazement, are able to see that she wears no underclothes at all during this performance! We have to denounce such appalling behaviour as totally subversive to all ideas of public morality and decency. We would urge that no respectable person, including any that claim to be gentlemen, should seek to experience this spectacle.

The upshot was that I was dispatched immediately to buy tickets for a performance where Lola Montez was appearing. I knew that there would be no chance of getting tickets to see her perform her spider dance. All those tickets had long since been bought by those who had professed, at reading about it, how shocked they were, and now wished to be further shocked at an actual performance.

With very little difficulty I bought tickets for an evening performance of "Lola Montez in Bavaria" at the Victoria Theatre. Having made my purchase, and having ignored the suggestive remarks of the impertinent young man who sold them to me, I much enjoyed walking along George Street, which, I had read, was as much like Bond Street in London as it is possible for one place to resemble another. It's true that I had several times to shake off a male importunate hand from those bucks who seemed to think that everyone shared their libertine view of Life. I did not dare even to look into the Café François, but hurried by with my tickets safely tucked away.

That evening, after a strong wind that blew most of the afternoon with some rain at times, we repaired to the theatre all eager to experience what we had heard so much about. I quite enjoyed the performance. Ma was more impressed with the actual theatre, which, I had to admit, had been constructed with that particular aim in mind. Several times I had to dig her discreetly in the ribs as she fell asleep. I knew that wine and dinner before the performance was a mistake.

Lola Montez was a most impressive actress, her sparkling contribution to the piece being well offset by the dull cast that accompanied her. I liked her. She was an attractive woman whose dark hair and almost jet black eyes certainly lent credence to her claim to be a Spanish noblewoman, but in my heart, having read about her more extensively than Ma, I knew she was in fact an impostor.

Afterwards I had to mollify the Leckies, especially Mr Leckie, who had expected something altogether more shocking, and therefore more enjoyable. I was accused of misleading them.

I pointed out that we were lucky to have seen a full performance for on a previous occasion there had been such a row in the theatre that Lola Montez had to appeal to the audience to stop. She asked the gentlemen in the pit and gallery not to interfere with the pleasures of others in the audience. She said, rather quaintly, that she liked a good row, but would the gentlemen respect the wishes of a lady and not interfere with the enjoyment of other people. I rather think that, as the players themselves were squabbling amongst themselves, the audience preferred a good row to a poor performance. Her calling herself a lady might have been seen as something of a joke, for by now her reputation had caught up with her!

My spirited defence made me less aware than I might have been at Ma's discomfiture. Something had upset her without any doubt. I made a note to myself by tying a knot in a kerchief to ask her about this when we were alone and had a quiet moment. Such moments were all too rare these days. Life seems to speed up as you get older and events seem just to whirl you along willy-nilly.

Chapter 8

A Ruined Evening

If anything at all typified the way things were between John Adam and Pip Pirrip, that incident at the theatre was a perfect example. Both these men had founded a thriving business that employed many men, and women, for women were increasingly being employed in firms in all sorts of positions. My friend, Elaine Pomeroy, for example, was in their main office, and had been for almost all her adult life. As I said, both men were supposed to be grown men with responsibilities, and just look how they behaved!

Ma was at her old game, finding me a beau. She pretended that John had insisted that we all go to the soiree together, where she was sure there would be a surfeit of suitable and eligible bachelors. John and Estella, who now went around openly, despite the wagging tongues, took us all, Phillip Gargery too, in their coach. John's position and lavish gifts to charities and business connections overcame many a man's scruples. Their wives might be scandalized, but business was business.

Ma, with my future in mind, had laid out some cash on the makings of a gown. Estella had helped choose the material, and we spent some time in deciding in what sort of style the new gown should be. In the end my choice was overruled by Estella, who wanted me to look gracious as well as inviting. She exclaimed that my figure was perfect for the new styles, and that my complexion, carefully protected as it had been by accident as I stayed indoors to read, than by design as became a respectable young woman, was set off to the utmost by the shade of green that we chose. Ma grumbled that green was unlucky. She also thought that it made me too pale, almost sickly. Her grumbling declined as the young men queued to asked for the favour of a dance.

I had several dances. Phillip Gargery drank too much, as usual, glowering at me as if he owned me. Oh! I liked him well enough, but I knew too well how his temper and drinking spoke against him. A foppish young man brought me back as it began over on the other side of the room. It was Pip Pirrip and John Adam arguing in public. It did not matter what they were arguing about, the point was that they were doing it in public and doing themselves and the firm no good as they did so. Elaine Pomeroy, my friend who worked at Adam and Pirrip, was there and saw it all.

At least that lump Phillip Gargery had his uses. Ma sent him over to see what was happening, and he shouldered his way through the crown, several young men being pushed to one side as he did so. I heard someone say 'Tasmanian Devil'. When he came back I was mortified. It was bad enough that John and Pip Pirrip were arguing in public, but now with John scarlet in the face from anger and red-splashed with wine, we heard that we had to leave. Estella, cool, as always, sent for our cloaks, as we had on this occasion decided that shawls were insufficient to cover our bare shoulders. My most recent dancing partner attempted to claim another dance. His hand around my waist he drew me out, but I stopped him with a look. In like fashion I withstood his requests for my address so that he might call upon me. Resisting the temptation to inform him that he was pursuing the daughter of a convict, for after all there was Ma beside me, and I did not wish to ruin her evening completely, I simply shook my head in what I hoped was a gracious gesture.

All this was not lost upon Phillip Gargery who had returned to tell us that our carriage had been brought round for us. To no-one's surprise, he said that he would not ride back with us, everybody supposing that he would stay to put away some more of the excellent drinks that were available. We adjusted ourselves in the carriage so that we made the least impact upon our dresses, for we ladies all hoped to be seen in them on some future occasion. I was glad that mine had no bustle, that item being one that was steadily falling into disfavour as women became more active.

Leaning out as we rounded the corner I saw Phillip Gargery for a moment in conversation with my former dancing partner. Then he was out of sight. I sank back and asked what the Tasmanian Devil was, only to find that I had created an embarrassed silence. This was filled by Ma, who was never at a loss for words with a remark upon the splendour of the scene from which we had just now departed. She declared that she had not never ever seen so many pretty women at one place together, and at the same, nor had she ever been so privileged before to have had the pleasure of seeing her only unmarried daughter so sought after by such eligible gentlemen. Her emphasis upon *unmarried and eligible* could scarcely be lost upon the company. I stayed silent for the remainder of the journey home, leaving the conversation to the others.

Chapter 10

The Hero!

Ma read in a newspaper that Pip was a hero. He had rescued people from a ship that was sinking. I asked Elaine, who was working at Adam and Pirrip, whether she knew anything about this. Elaine Pomeroy was the sort of young woman who couldn't keep anything to herself, so she readily passed on the facts to me, first telling me that she was, of course, sworn to secrecy, so I was not to tell anyone else.

Elaine had assisted in making arrangements for Pip to do a tour of the outlying offices of Adam and Pirrip. She thought that he had been forced to do it as they were all getting slack. Amongst other bookings she had booked a place for him on the SS Georgette. This was the ship that had sunk, and although a young woman had helped Pip, he had more or less saved everyone. This all came to light when a survivor of the wreck had come to Sydney seeking the man who had saved everyone. This was Pip, of course. Elaine took this man to Pip, who having accepted his thanks, had sworn Elaine to secrecy.

Elaine took the man to a nearby coffee house and got the whole story from him. He told her that the account in the newspaper was basically correct; they were calling the girl involved "Western Australia's Grace Darling". But it was Pip who had stayed on the ship until the last moment, making sure that everyone who could be saved was saved. The girl, who had ridden a horse into the sea, had certainly done her best, but it was Pip, in this man's estimation, who was the unsung hero. This man then told Elaine that, amongst others, Pip had saved a young woman, a celebrated actress, no less!   She was Maria De Lasseps and was doing monologue performances about the sinking at a small theatre in Sydney.

I bought a newspaper to read about it. Ma never bought one, preferring to read one that others had bought and discarded. She said that just because a newspaper had been read didn't alter the news within it. She also used to say that what can't speak can't lie, but I doubted that very much, and preferred to take all that I read in the newspapers with a pinch of salt. Turning to the back pages I found an advertisement, and I cut it out.

I still have it.

Drama

Patrons of the arts, and those seeking to enjoy a noble and uplifting experience are invited to a dramatic performance, where the true story of **The Truly Heroic and Shocking Story of the Fateful End of the Steamship Georgette** will be told by that well known actress: **Maria De Lasseps**

who is fresh from her success estime in Melbourne.

Miss De Lasseps, who suffered herself in this cruel episode, is willing to put aside her pain and anguish to bring to her public, the truth.

Once I had shown this to Ma she was desperate to see the performance. I too was intrigued. Perhaps the man that I had once thought to be a villain had some redeeming features. Elaine said that she could get seats for us all at what she thought would be a packed house. I was not really surprised however when we entered a very small establishment to find that we three people and just about two dozen others made up the entire audience.

I thought that the performance by Miss De Lasseps much less interesting than had been promised by the advertisement. I had heard more stimulating tales told by Elaine who, on occasions, kept both Ma and me fully entertained by stories of what went on behind the scenes in the offices of Adam and Pirrip. All conveyed to us in complete confidence, of course. I contained my impatience while a silly girl made wind noises and thunder in the wings and Maria finished the first part of her show. Elaine had told me that we could meet Maria privately in the interval.

We did so. I was not impressed, as I quickly saw through the picture that this third rate actress was trying to show us of herself. An actress by inclination, if not by ability, she seemed unable to live in any way other than an imaginary world of her own. Both Elaine and Ma were enthralled. They loved a show of any sort, whilst I preferred more ability and substance. "Macbeth" or the Scottish play, as Miss De Lasseps would have described it, no doubt playing the part of third witch, was much more what I would have elected to have entertained me. However, I was here seeking the truth, so I dutifully sat through an equally dull and turgid second half, after which we were joined by the great actress herself and took ourselves off to a common eating-house, where she attacked her food with not a little sound and fury.

Mary Lassy, which was Miss De Lasseps real name, also downed several glasses of wine, explaining that it had been held by all the notable doctors that wine was good for the vocal chords, that part of the body upon which she depended to make her way in the world. Elaine nearly choked on her chop having heard this, so I quickly turned the conversation to the hero of her show.

With food and drink inside her, Mary became more thoughtful and less theatrical. Her account of what she had seen and experienced, now had a frankness that was lacking before. She freely admitted that she had allowed her experiences to be elaborated upon somewhat by her dramatic imagination, but insisted that Pip had indeed played a major part in the rescues and that only the fact that a young woman had upstaged him meant that the newspapers had concentrated on her rather than on him. It's always the case, she explained. A pretty young woman, here she paused to let it sink in that we were in the presence of such a being, is a magnetic draw.

Chapter 11

The Picnic

It was John who insisted that we all went. To be honest, I would sooner have stayed at home, but Ma was so keen to see her betters, and to show me off. I think she thought that I might make a catch of some earl or lord. Even an esquire would have pleased her. John wanted to be seen. He always wanted to be in the front ranks, even if they were only the ranks of the self-made. He was friendly with the Thornes who had arranged for him to bring a party. Naturally John had been expected to put his hand within his purse, and to be fair to him, he never stinted to do that. To John the occasion was an opportunity, not only to be seen, but also to do some business, and the further up the persons attending were on the social ladder, the better.

Ma loved these sort of occasions, taking the opportunity to spot someone whom she knew from the old days who was, in fact, no better than she. They never discussed the old days. It was as if a pact had been decided that if one did not betray a past, then all the others followed suit. She grumbled at having to eat out in the open air at a picnic, but was surprised, as indeed I was, to find that the food was quite good. And it was served in tents. She managed to put away several glasses of Champagne, encouraged by John. Estella, I noted, ate sparingly, and drank very moderately. I resolved to emulate her example in future.

There was some talk of a camera to record the occasion, and John, ever eager to gain some publicity, drew as near as was possible, hoping to be amongst the group who might figure in a pictorial record of this pleasant occasion. He was unable to get too close as several equerries made sure that the prince had a space about him at all times into which no-one was allowed to intrude unless he desired it. It was notable that several single attractive young women seemed to be able to enter this magic area with ease.

I retreated to the shade, seeking to keep cool in a dress that might have set off my figure and flattered my complexion (Ma's description) but was way too hot for this time of the year. At the very edges of the beach I saw some urchins going in and out of the water. They seemed so cool. They were chased off eventually. I was watching them and so missed what happened next and had to rely upon John's account of the attack upon the prince's life. As if that were not drama enough, John's friend, Mr Thorne, was shot in the leg or foot, to the distress of his wife and daughter who saw it all.

We were all hurried away, and had to make out what had really transpired from the newspapers in the following days. These reported that the prince was not badly hurt, and received excellent care from the Nightingale nurses. I was seized with envy at the opportunities that were afforded these young women. Trained in England in the very latest nursing techniques, that I heard had been developed in the Crimea, they came ready to work alongside doctors. Both medicine and nursing were considered to be, in my eyes at least, the noblest of the professions. I ignored ignorant comments to the effect that nursing was not a profession, but just an occupation.

When I later talked to Ma about this event she declared that she had not been one of our party! She maintained doggedly that she had remained at home, and that I was confused as to her whereabouts because I was so addled in my mind as to wish to become a nurse. I really cannot be sure whether my aspirations had so upset her that she truly forgot, or whether this was the first intimation that her mind was changing as she grew older. I looked at her keenly. She was a little more stooped, a little more breathless and a little more unready to try new things. It manifested itself in small ways. Coaxed to try some new dish, she would aver that she preferred a piece of bread and cheese.

Chapter 12

Death of Estella

What annoyed me most about the whole affair was the calm way in which everyone assumed that nurses would blindly accept the bidding of doctors. I had read so much of how nursing was becoming more professional, thanks to Miss Nightingale's efforts in the Crimean War, and later on in England, that I thought that nurses were listened to now. It seems that I was wrong, but it will change, it really will.

When Jamie came back from the hospital and told us what had happened, and how he had been sent packing by a nurse, I knew that she had only done so because some doctor had decreed it. Elaine had had to spend some time in hospital, and told me how the poor nurses were ordered around something shocking, to use her words. I think that it was probably this event that helped me make up my mind to try my luck at getting trained as a nurse. I was still single and well read, if not educated to the extent that Jamie was.

I wrote a letter in my best handwriting, which, to my delight, was answered. I was requested to present myself at the hospital along with two written testimonials from persons of note. That gave me pause. Who could I possibly get to do that? Eventually a parson who knew us, and a rich businessman, whose son I had spurned at a ball, wrote a few lines. I thanked them only to hear that the parson considered me so godless that were I to be selected for training I would be removed from his parish where he considered that I was a most unhealthy influence upon other younger women; while the rich business man was glad to see the back of that young hussy who had the temerity to lead his son on, and then reject him.

It was Elaine who conveyed these sentiments to me. She added, as she did so, that she did so from the kindliest and friendliest of reasons as she did not wish me to be unduly upset were I not to be selected for something upon which I had so obviously set my heart.

When I attended my interview I looked around and I considered that of all the young women waiting to be seen, I was the most presentable. On being called in I sat down, only to be rebuked for so doing when I had yet to be told to. I'm afraid that this upset me, and I must have shown it, for I was asked whether I was used to being instructed, or whether I had always done as I wished. I cannot quite remember my reply, but it must have satisfied them for they continued to question me. As I answered all the questions of the persons who sat the other side of a highly polished table, who seemed so very cold and inhuman, my confidence drained away.

Waiting for an answer was a torment. During that time Phillip Gargery made himself objectionable to me by seeking me out on every conceivable occasion until, in exasperation, I told him to speak as to what was upon his mind. This opened the floodgates of a verbal attack upon the way that I treated him, the fashion in which I neglected his feelings and that he was determined that he would take no more of such callous treatment. His spleen thoroughly vented, he grew less angry and asked whether he had any chance that I might look favourably upon an offer of marriage from him?

I knew that this was coming and I had an answer that I had rehearsed mentally for some time. It was merely a rewording of the answer that I had given several other suitors, much to Ma's dismay. However, just as I was about to launch into this, he stopped me.

"Do think of Jamie and Amos. They might be very disappointed if you say no, for I shall have to speak to your Ma, and when I do so I shall not be able to hide what I know about that friendship."

Of course, I knew how very close they were. Naturally, they were discreet, so discreet that Ma did not suspect a thing. She would have liked to see him married, but was prepared for him to knock about with his mates until the right girl came along. He had quite a few young women that he and Amos went about with, but none that he was as close to as he was to Amos Bulstrode. I said nothing about any of this. If there was one rule that came first, it was that the least said in any situation the better.

Playing for time, I told Phillip Gargery that I had applied to be a nurse, and that when I started my training I would have to be unmarried. I added that as soon as I heard that I was accepted, I would tell him.

"But what if they do not accept you, what then, eh?"

Reluctantly I had to admit that I would be free to marry.

"Then, if you are not accepted, can I take it that you will accept my proposal?"

I was tired. He was wearing me down. I thought that I would be accepted, so I said 'yes'. What a mistake! In two days I heard that they had carefully considered my application, but were sorry to have to inform me that I was not considered suitable. To say that I was furious would be to understate the situation completely. I was livid. I was a flaming volcano of anger. How dare they refuse me? Everyone and anyone was now the target of my anger. If I could not say how ill-used I was to the faces of those smug, self-satisfied beings who derided me for daring to sit in their presence, then I would be angry with anyone who crossed my path.

Surprisingly, Phillip Gargery was sympathetic. He listened to me as I recounted again and again how I had been humiliated. He took my hand and then when, eventually I cried, he wiped away my tears and said:

"Never mind them. Marry me. That'll show them."

"Show them what?"

"That they are fools to reject you when someone like me loves you."

My pride was hurt. Marrying Phillip Gargery would indeed show the world that I was not totally rejected. Looking back, I realise now, how I had been trapped by my feelings. I should have slept on my answer, but Amos looked in at that very moment, seeking Jamie. As he admired himself in our mirror, Phillip Gargery, seeing him, caught my eye and lifted an eyebrow. I gave in. We went to tell Ma.

Chapter 13

Satis Novis Achieved and John Marries

It just seemed so unjust to me. Ma was cock-o-hoop over the whole thing. There was Pip Pirrip, mooning about, and only just about pulling his weight in the firm, when suddenly John spurs him into action and gets him his lost inheritance! Elaine was of the opinion that the lawyers in the case had sailed mightily near the wind in order to achieve this result. She made the gesture of rubbing her forefinger and thumb together saying that something had changed hands.

I went home, still upset about the whole affair, only to find my husband home from work plying Ma with drink to make her talk. There they sat, both having worked their way through several bottles, and Ma obviously intoxicated. I was infuriated. It was bad enough to have a husband who put drink before work, but when he used alcohol on my mother in order to wheedle secrets from her, it made me livid. I took him outside to tell him what I had heard from Elaine.

At least Pip Pirrip used some of his inheritance to good effect. Having some land, he caused to have constructed upon it a tolerably fair sort of house, and used Jamie, Amos and Phillip, amongst others to build it for him. By now there was no shortage of architects. Many had come from England, but just as many had grown up in this country and knew how to build something that was adapted to the sort of climate that we had. So, apart from some dramatic views, Satis Novis House had a wide veranda, cool rooms and a modern kitchen where his resident cook could prepare excellent meals. Ma, of course, usually declined any new dish, saying that she was a simple body who liked simple food.

It was the same story when John got married. She turned up her nose at the strange dishes that were served after the ceremony in John's new house.

After being seen all round the town with practically every respectable marriageable woman available, and some who were considerably less respectable, John announced that he was to marry. The woman, an Italian immigrant, who told everyone that she was related to Garibaldi, turned John's head by persuading him that no-one who was not immediately related to nobility (she also claimed a kinship with the Bourbons, and John believed her) was suitable for him. I'm still not sure that John believed all this nonsense. He did like to cut a dash, and act the swell, so a grand marriage was very much to his taste.

We all went to see them married in the Catholic Cathedral, and I was not surprised when very soon after Marietta was brought to bed by a fine boy. It had been quite apparent to anyone who had eyes that her wedding gown was quite tight in front and that her gait was that of a woman who carried more than her usual share of plumpness. Her declining to dance at the wedding breakfast determined in Ma's eyes that all of our suspicions were probably correct.

From the moment that I set eyes upon her I knew exactly who she resembled. That brown curly hair, those regular pearl-like teeth that were revealed when she opened her tiny, perfectly shaped mouth. And the eyes, the eyes! So wonderfully expressive, especially when she vented her anger, real or feigned. It was Lola all over again. I had so often seen pictures of Lola Montez in the newspapers I just could not be wrong. Indeed I had seen her on the stage, and so had Ma who agreed with me when I pointed it out. 'Another foreign bitch' was her response.

Despite that, and the fact that she recoiled from Ma as she was presented to her, muttering something in Italian, which later someone said was to do with the evil eye, we all had the most tremendous time. Most of John's employees in the Sydney office were there, including Elaine, who thereafter was my main source of information about Mrs Marietta Adams, nee Rossi. According to Elaine, She led John a dog's life, spending money as if there was no end to where it might come from. As to the little boy, Federico Guiseppe, or little Freddy, as they called him when he was not around, he was spoiled to such an extent that, far from being a likeable little lad, he was a pest. He could draw though, so they used to give him paper and pencil to occupy himself with whenever he was brought to the office. It amused everyone when he did drawings of the staff that were tolerably accurate, though not always that flattering!

With Ma in a huff and Jamie and Amos quarrelling, I left them to it and went to dance. When I got back it was to find Ma in tears. It was obvious that Jamie and Amos had upset her. I spoke sharply to them, telling them that they should have more respect for her at her age. Neither of them replied which enraged me. I was about to demand an explanation when Phillip, much the worse for drink of course, arrived demanding that we go home. He insisted that he couldn't take a moment more of what he called this charade. We were all subdued in the carriage,

At Pip's invitation we rode over to Satis Novis, the house that he had built for himself when he came into his inheritance. He welcomed us extravagantly with champagne. He told us that he and John drank a great deal of that wine when they were in the goldfields. I didn't like it, nor did Phillip, he preferring something stronger, and I found it too dry for my taste. I prefer sherry wine or port wine.

"I have always wanted to see you wed ever since you came to Sydney. I nursed secret hopes of romance for myself, as you probably guessed, with a lady who is no longer with us. But just because my hopes of marital harmony were not realised it does not mean that you two cannot achieve that. God bless you both."

We all walked around the house admiring the way in which it had been decorated. He moved much slower than he used to, and I heard him catch his breath from time to time. I spotted a walking stick that was propped against a chair on the veranda. I wondered whether he really needed it or was it just a part of him being a gentleman? Unlike John, he still had a full head of hair. He never spoke of John's help in achieving his inheritance from Magwitch. I wondered if he knew that John had married?

Finally we stopped at a fireplace where, above the elaborate marble mantle that must have cost more than our rent for a year, there were two ugly Chinese pottery pieces.

"I was given those by a Celestial, a Chinaman, who I once helped. It seems that if you help a Chinaman to save his life he considers that his life is forfeit to you. He pressed me to take these pieces that had some sort of religious significance to him. It was by giving me these that he seemed to think that he was releasing himself from that obligation. Now I should like you to have them as a wedding present."

Naturally I tried to look grateful. Some money would have been more use. It didn't please Phillip either, but he held his tongue, put it into the carriage, and we took it home.

Our ride home in the carriage through the January heat, despite it being late in the evening, was not a pleasant one. Ma kept up a stream of remarks upon the house, how spacious it was, how well sited, with such pleasant views. And how suitable it was for a gentleman. This last remark was obviously directed at my husband who every day these days exhibited behaviour that fell well out the boundaries of decent behaviour expected of a gentleman.

He was sullen, as he so often was after drinking. I knew better than to comment how much he had put away at Satis Novis. Nevertheless, my silence was taken by him as agreement to all that Ma said. So it was no surprise that on reaching home, he quickly took the china upstairs and put it into the attic. At least we were in agreement with that course of action. It was also no surprise when he said that he wanted to go out for a drink.

Having been out all day I wished to stay quietly at home, but Phillip insisted that he wanted to go out, so I said that he had better go by himself. I'm afraid that this how he spends his time now. Even when he's working he drinks before he comes home. I sometimes wished that I had not been persuaded into this marriage.

Chapter 14

Being Married

The other thing that had persuaded me to marry was the fact that James Barnet's Garden Palace was going to be constructed in the Botanic Gardens. It had to be finished ready for the 1879 Sydney international Exhibition so they needed lots of men. Phillip Gargery went down there, but they knew too much about his reputation and turned him away. I tried to get the firm interested in proposing Pip as a worker, for Adam and Pirrip it was a great opportunity to garner some very lucrative contracts. Elaine did her best, but had to admit defeat.

Pip complained to me about prejudice.

"It's your own fault. Everyone knows you drink."

"Everyone I know drinks."

"Not everyone drinks until they fall down, unless they get in a fight first and knock someone else down like you do."

"But Livvy, they need people like me with experience in working iron. I'm a specialist."

"They don't need specialist drunks."

"You judge me so harshly. Stop judging me and tell me what I should do to get a job."

I pushed a newspaper towards him, tapping with my finger to indicate the passage about the use of electricity that was going to be put in place to speed up the work.

"Now this will require real specialist knowledge. Try to learn something about this new electricity and use it to your advantage."

"How do I do that?"

I went into the shop and gathered together some books on generating electricity. They were by Michael Faraday and Sir Humphry Davey.

"Start with these."

I watched as he sullenly opened one and began to read.

I went away, not sure that he would stick to the task that I had set him. When I came back with some tea later, it pleased me mightily to see that he was still reading.

" I can't make head not tail of this Liv."

"What part are you reading?"

"This stuff on arc lamps."

He looked at me and said:

"The principle of the arc light, is that when you put two carbon rods in a circuit, and they are brought together, an arc is created. This arc gives off a brilliant incandescence, an extremely bright light, which can be kept going for as long as the rods that are in the circuit are just separated enough, and kept mechanically fed in this fashion, to maintain the arc."

"Wait a moment. You're not reading that."

"No. It's what I've just read."

"What do you mean, *what you've just read* ?"

He looked at me. He explained slowly, as one would to a child, that he remembered what he read.

I must have looked amazed.

"I just remember it. If I read something carefully, I remember what I have read. Doesn't everyone?"

I took the book from him, and turned the pages until I reached the section on generators, and pushed it back to him.

"Read that. No, not aloud."

I watched as he carefully read the paragraph that I had shown him, and then I took the book away. I waited expectantly. We looked at each other.

"Well?"

"Oh! I see.

Looking at the corner of the room he recited the passage absolutely word perfect.

"But I don't know what it means Liv."

"Don't worry about that, just read the passages that I mark for you. When you repeat them to me I will explain them. Once you have done this you can ask for a job and they are bound to be impressed at what you know. They are also bound to have real experts bringing the equipment from England for you to work with."

I was right, the electric light stuff all came from England, and was installed by men who came with them. They were pleased to have a labourer who seemed to know what it was that they were doing. And so Phillip Gargery was employable again. I began to hear, however, that he was still drinking when he thought no one was around to observe him.

Chapter 16

He's Gone

Toby must have been drinking, most unusual for him. He had been in town and was returned, looking bedraggled. I saw mud on one knee of his best britches. He gestured to me, taking off his hat. I noticed that his hair was thinning. He looked older. He was older. I walked towards him, but as I did so he retreated before me still keeping his eyes on me until we were both outside the shop. He stirred the black boy with his foot who, making a mewing sound, slid over sideways, then crawled away.

Looking furtive, he spoke in such a low tone that I had the utmost difficulty in determining what he was saying.

"I'm sorry Olivia."

I kept calm. It is ever my nature to do so, and my habitual sang froid did not desert me. I knew that it would be about my husband. Wasn't it always? I waited, pulling my shawl about me. Sometimes in the evenings it could be cold. Well, it was July.

Toby swallowed. I had never in all my life seen him so nervous. This must be bad.

"He's gone," he began in a rush.

Now having started, words gushed out like water from a pump, his emotions pumping them in a steady stream.

"He had to go. He killed a man, fighting. He was drinking again despite what he said. I saw it all. He's run off, afraid to face the consequences. The police..."

I interrupted him.

"What happened? Tell me exactly."

"He picked a fight after getting drunk in a drinking house down by the docks. I think he had been working there all day, in the docks, that is. You know what he's like once he's had a few. He can't stop until he passes out. This time he got savage, and I really mean savage. He picked on a complete stranger and challenged him to fight. He tried to laugh it off, and that made him angry. So angry that he beat him until he died. He beat him to death. He's gone into hiding.

"Where?"

He spread his hand that shook slightly, to indicate that he knew no more.

"Couldn't you help him?"

Toby looked confused.

"I was there. I was having a dram and I heard the shouting. I went to see and found out that it was him."

"So, we can expect the police here, looking for him?

"No."

"No?"

"He gave a false name to the police first off, then when his mates pushed over the police, he ran off."

I thanked Toby for telling what had happened. He smiled. Not the smile of a man who did what he should have done and was pleased to have that acknowledged. But a more secretive smile of a man who knew more than he had told. In time I would get the rest of the story. In the meantime Ma would have to know, but not yet awhiles.

Chapter 17

Ma Rambles and Toby proposes

It was Ma's screams that woke me. I was having a bit of a lie down in the back bedroom where it's cooler and not so noisy, although you can always hear the birds. They never seem to stop even in the heat of the day. I smelled the smoke immediately I opened the door and ran down the stairs losing a shoe as I did so, my heart beating like all the regimental drums. Ma was in a chair, her hair and front of her dress and apron all wet and her cap askew. Some wet newspaper and a candle were on the floor where Lizbeth looked up at me as she mopped the floor with one of our best towels.

"Sorry. I panicked."

"You all right Ma?"

I found another towel and dried her hair. Lizbeth went off and I heard her telling Toby what had happened.

"I couldn't see. I wanted to read the paper."

A week later Mrs Jones brought her back home again.

"She was looking for her mistress. She told me that she had been arrested."

"Thank you. At least it makes a change from her looking for Jamie! Her husband, my Pa, dead and buried long since."

This was becoming increasingly common. Usually she was just asking passers-by where Jamie had gone. She was more and more living in the past. But now she had taken to looking for him and wandering off to do so. I was getting afraid that she might be put away. Someone mentioned the Lunatic Asylum at Parramatta.

What with one thing and another I was so taken up with my problems that I was a mite surprised when Toby asked if he could speak to me in private. I had known him for years and I knew that he had always wanted to marry me, but I thought that I had put a stop to all that when I married Phillip Gargery. Now, however, he was looking serious, and sure enough he was proposing that we made a match. To my reply that I was married he asked when I had last seen or heard from my husband?

I said that was not an issue. In the eyes of the law I was married wherever my husband was. He got excited and wanted to know if I proposed to throw the rest of my life away? I told him that he presumed too much on our relationship. In any case I said that I scarcely thought that I was throwing my life away, and even if that were indeed the situation, which it was not, it was no business of his.

He returned to his work, the set of his shoulders telling me that he had hoped for a different answer from me. I should have known that it wouldn't stop there. Sure enough, he was back. This time it was on another tack.

Chapter 19

We Lose the Shop and I Begin to Work

He smiled nervously. He had changed his clothes. He looked different, quite foreign. I sat down and put down the books that I was packing up to send off. The scissors and brown paper slid off the bench. I knew Toby well enough to recognise that if he wished to talk to me it would be something that he had prepared. Ever since I had sent him packing after his proposal I had expected something of this kind. He had a bundle of papers in his hands that trembled as he laid them carefully on the table between us. I ignored them, waiting for him to speak.

"It's bad news. We are not only not making money, but we are actually losing it. Look. Here are the figures."

"But we still have customers"

"Not so many."

"But we still have them."

"Yes, but they don't buy as much. And no one buys Jamies' bookcases. No-one wants something so well finished when they can find something altogether cheaper, even if it is inferior."

"What about that Government contract to supply furniture to the observatory and other places?"

"We lost it. We were undercut. Look I have the letters from William Scott."

" So what are we to do?"

He licked his lips. His eyes slid sideways to where Lizbeth was minding an empty shop. He lowered his voice.

"We are really in a very poor way, a very bad state. Most of our stock still has to be paid for. Our rent is overdue. Our sales are down. I would have drawn your attention to this before but you have been so involved in dealing with your Ma."

"Yes, yes, but what must we do?"

My voice came out shriller than I had intended.

Now he looked shifty. He would not look straight at me. Instead he fiddled with the papers, straightening them, pushing at them to get them even neater than they were already. I reached over and took them from him. I raised my eyebrows in question. I could not trust my voice.

"Everything has got worse since your husband.....er went. I have a proposal, or rather a set of proposals that in my humble opinion will assist us. I have written them down."

He drew another paper from an inside pocket and unfolded it. His hands trembled as he smoothed out the creases, then he pushed it towards me. I didn't want to pick it up. He stood up abruptly, sweat glistening on his balding head. He had drawn his hair over to cover his baldness. His stool fell over, and lizbeth looked towards us wondering at the noise.

"Olivia."

I gave him my basilisk look. He grew paler.

"I'm sorry. Mrs Gargery. I will leave you. You can read what I am suggesting in peace, at your leisure, without interruption."

My look brought him to a stop. He went to join Lizbeth.

I drew the paper towards me. I read it. It was really very simple. There were only four lines on it.

1. Move to a smaller premises.
2. Stop selling Jamie's bookshelves.
3. Find a home for Mrs O'Brian.
4. Stop employing Lizbeth

Apart from the list that he had given me there were other papers, and from them I could readily see that we were really in as bad a way as was possible to be. I determined to say little of this to Ma. Instead, after some days I called in Toby and said that I could see from the figures that he had provided, that he was right. We had to take action, and I should have to do it soon if we were to save anything from the wreck that was our business.

He licked his lips and said that he had a suggestion to make. I sat tired and disheartened. I nodded for him to go on. His proposal was that he should take over the business, give us enough cash to move to a small house, and pay us something each week until I found employment. Had I not been so tired and depressed I would have been more alert and wanted to know where he had the money to pay us. I might also have wanted to know if we could not make it pay, how could he?

But, as I said, I was tired, Ma had been particularly troublesome, I was tired, and it seemed a way out of the morass into which I felt we were slipping. I agreed. Telling Ma that we were moving somewhere new that she would like was an easy lie, for the small house where we finished up did indeed please her. It was more convenient in all sorts of ways, including piped water and a water closet. Without actually saying so, I intimated to her that Toby was to look after business for us. I hid the fact that it was ours no longer. To my intense surprise she accepted all these changes, saying that at her age it was right to let others do the work and right for her to take her ease. She added rather grandly that she had been considering for some time that she ought to retire and live a much less busy life.

"After working so hard I really think that I deserve at last to live on the fruits of my labours."

Everyone knew about the place, it seemed, how it had started and then been changed. All I knew was what Ma had told me about when she had been there, and that was precious little. She seemed to shrink down into herself when I said that I was going to work there. I tried to show her the letter that I had received saying that I was offered employment in the newly established Industrial and Training School for Girls. She ignored it, even when I left it on the table in our new home. I folded it up and went to see the place. It was certainly grim, but at least it offered wayward girls some shelter and a chance to redeem themselves. The work that I was to do as an overseer was simple enough.

It was Lizbeth who came to see us in our new quarters who told me why my mother was so upset.

"She thinks that you mean to put her into the lunatic asylum. Paramatta Asylum is where all the loonies end up when their folks can't or won't care for them any more."

"It's not an asylum any more. And whatever gave her the idea that I was going to put her away?"

She looked shifty and fiddled with her shawl. I asked outright:

"Did you tell her that?"

She looked shocked, and quickly told me how she had overheard Toby telling me that we could no longer run the shop. She had then tackled him as she had also heard that she was to lose her place.

"He said that you couldn't make the shop pay, that I was to be got rid of, and your Ma was to be put away. He was right about the shop and me, so I thought that he was right about your Ma.

"So, did you tell her that I was going to put her away?"

"Not exactly."

So, what did you say?"

Lizbeth began to cry. She pulled a handkerchief out of her reticule and sniffed into it.

"Oh Olivia, you have always been so hard on a body. I can't just remember in so many words, but I might, just might, mind you, have said that you were planning to make sure that she was taken care of, looked after. Oh! I just can't call the exact words to mind. Anyway, you must ask Toby for he certainly made it clear to her once you had signed over the shop to him, which, by the by, is doing well now."

I knew already that it was prospering and I also knew why. When Toby had persuaded me that the shop was not going to be successful, and had encouraged me to make it over to him he had done so knowing that there was something valuable in the shop that he could sell. It was two old books that had been brought from England. Because I had signed everything over to him, he was the legal owner of them, so I had no way of getting them back. Indeed I only found out what he had done when a representative came to see me about them. They knew that they had come from our shop and wished to know whether I had any similar books.

To add to our woes, my brother, Jamie had been persuaded that a much better opportunity awaited him on the other side of Australia. They were to build a cathedral in Perth, and he and his mate, Amos Bulstrode, had been offered work on it, as they needed skilled joiners. Jamie had been told that there was at least ten years' work to be had there. It was too good an opportunity to be missed. It might be a long ways off but the rewards could be tremendous. I was dismayed. Ma could not comprehend the enormous distances involved and reassured me that his master would allow him to come home from time to time. She thought he was still an apprentice.

Suddenly I realised that I was losing everyone I knew. Estella was dead. My husband had disappeared again, and now Jamie was proposing to leave us. The only one left from the old days was Lizbeth. She had not married a lord as she intended. I clearly remember her saying that this was what wanted. Well, as Ma used to say: 'if you don't get what you want, you must want what you've got.' She got someone who was no lord, but was, instead, a steady dependable man, never out of employment.

"Oh! He's such a dull dog. He's such a dear soul though, so I can't complain."

Chapter 21

Not a Stranger

It was the beard and the hat that was pulled low that fooled my senses and made me indifferent to the stranger's presence. I carried on talking, my arm linked in Lizbeth's, as we strolled away from the theatre. The stranger turned away, striding down the pavement, and it was only then that I recognised the gait and the way in which he hunched his shoulders as if to protect himself, whilst ready to lash out a blow against an opponent. Lizbeth felt me grow tense and asked:

"What's the matter?"

"Nothing. I thought I saw, but no. Let's go home."

At home, after making sure that Ma was safe and letting the girl go who was minding her, I relaxed a little as we had a glass of wine. This was becoming a ritual now at the end of a busy day. And why not? It was not that easy to hold everything together, and a glass of wine helped me to a state of ease where I could stumble to my solitary bed and get the solace of a good night's sleep. Ma always slept well. A dose of her usual helped her, and drove away whatever demons she struggled with every day.

Lizbeth poured another and I took it readily while she spoke about staying with me. I told her not to be so foolish. She should go home where her husband would be waiting for her. She made a face at this, but still took her shawl and bonnet and let herself out. I must have dozed off. The noise that woke me was not that loud; it was enough however to remind me that I should have locked up when Lizbeth went. I stood up.

Before me stood Toby. He had been drinking. He was sweating and unsteady and I could see that he meant mischief. Ever since that day when I had confronted him about the way he had cheated us out of our rightful dues I had been aware that he might try to get back at me.

"So Lizbeth is gone?"

I said nothing but my eyes slid to the poker in the grate. Toby saw my eyes move and forestalled me by picking it up. He flung it into the corner. I winced at the sound.

"That means that we are quite alone. I know your Ma is upstairs asleep, but she won't bother us will she? Your medicine that you give her every night means that she will stay in a drugged state for some while yet."

I tried to keep my voice steady.

"Go away Toby before someone finds you here and you get into real trouble."

"I told you that I would not let you rest. You will do as I tell you."

He spoke in a deliberate tone that made me begin to be ever more fearful.

The door opened. We both looked at it. In looking he turned and revealed something that glinted in his hand. Lizbeth came in, even as I screamed in my head: 'go away'.

"I left my programme. I forgot it. Why Toby, whatever are you doing here?"

Putting something shining to her neck, he answered:

" I'm settling old scores."

Lizbeth stood still. She smiled at me. I asked myself, what on earth has she got to smile about? The door began to open slowly and the stranger eased into the room. Removing his hat, he revealed himself as no stranger. Despite the beard we all recognised Phillip Gargery.

"Put it down Toby. Put it down, <u>now</u>."

Toby hesitated and reluctantly dropped his hand letting the knife fall where it tinkled prettily into the grate. With one blow from Pip, Toby was smashed into the sideboard then fell sideways and we all heard the best glasses ringing against each other inside. He tried to get up, raised his head, and then slumped back.

"My God! You've killed him."

"Not so. He'll live and tell you how he made me run away."

With some water in his face, Toby was revived and did indeed confirm Phillip Gargery's story. Toby had paid money to someone to challenge Pip. He fought with the challenger, then, thinking that he had killed him, fled to live in the countryside under an assumed name. It was Toby who told my husband, Pip, to run away. The opponent was not dead, merely acting dead under instructions. Toby had conceived this plan, when seeing Pip knock someone down who had seemed to die, but had been revived.

I sent Lizbeth to make sure that the front door was locked and bolted, then I told Toby to sit down and I asked him why he had done this.

"Ever since I came to work for your Ma and Pa I was a slave, a slave to you Olivia; and you ignored me. In the beginning, as you grew up, I expected this. Then as you grew older you didn't change, but as you were cold and heartless to all the other men, I didn't mind. As long as I could be near you I was satisfied. I knew that I would never ever achieve my dream of marrying you, but then, no one else would, so I didn't mind that either. Seeing you each day gave me a satisfaction that you cannot imagine. Sometimes, when I did something that pleased you, you smiled at me and I walked around in a daze of happiness.

Then you, Phillip Gargery, came along, only to be ignored as all the others had been, and seeing your frustration gave me even more pleasure. So I took pleasure in others displeasure? It made me happy and enabled me to continue. It gave me even more pleasure when you revealed that you were a waster and a drunkard."

Phillip's colour rose and he went to rise but I restrained him.

"Let us hear him out."

Toby looked at the floor and spoke bitterly.

"So a wastrel and drunkard married the woman that I had been worshipping. What was I expected to do? Congratulate you both?"

He shook his head. He looked straight at me.

"You know that when your husband fled I tried to use that to my advantage. You refused me. You know that I stole from you, and that I lied to get the shop from you. What else was left to me? I couldn't have you, and the shop was all the life that I had otherwise. Without that I was nothing. I would have willingly left you alone, had I not heard that Phillip Gargery was returned. I knew that once he came to you he would find out from you what I had done, so I determined to make it impossible for him to gain that knowledge. You can see, can't you that I had no other choice."

We had all been so intent on listening to Toby that we forgot to watch him carefully, so when he suddenly jumped up, pushing Lizbeth down and kicking over his chair, he was nearly able to run straight out of the room. Phillip grappled with him and would have caught him fast by his overcoat, had I not, in lifting Lizbeth, got in his way. Toby wriggled out of his overcoat and was through the door, slamming it in our faces. We heard his feet on the bare wooden stairs. By the time that we had wrestled the door open he was half way up.

"Ma!" I gasped.

Jostling each other we somehow managed to scramble upstairs where we found an open window and Ma in her nightgown.

"Where's my Jamie?" she demanded.

"You were hiding him from me. Why has he gone out the window?"

Phillip Gargery looked out of the window. He went to climb out. I pulled at his coat.

"For God's sake, no. Stop. Let him go."

Phillip shook his head. He pulled away from me and climbed through the casement and stood on the windowsill. Pulling himself up by holding onto the gutter he managed to get onto the lower slopes of the roof. A tile slid by him and fell into the yard with what seemed to be a big enough crash to awaken everyone in the neighbourhood. Looking up I could make out two forms that grew clearer as my eyes grew more used to the darkness. One of them slithered along the top until he reached the smokestack.

Phillip shouted at Toby. The two forms suddenly became one before they parted and one slid down to the gutter where it stopped. There a pause and a hand slowly appeared from above moving towards the form. It reached it, but as it did so, the body plunged over the edge into our yard.

Ma was hysterical and kept shouting that someone had killed her Jamie. Lizbeth took her back to her room and gave her a dose of the usual. I ran downstairs with Phillip close behind me. Our neighbours were in the yard, some had lights, but in the confusion it was difficult to tell just who was there.

I told Phillip to go, pushing him out of the yard. He nodded, understanding, then turned back.

"Buck Street."

"What?"

"Nineteen Buck Street."

"Yes, I understand. Now for God's sake go."

Two days later, at that address, we met, and agreed that he should disappear again for a while until all these events had become history. Our parting however was not so sudden that I was not able to take the opportunity to show Mr Phillip Gargery that his wife did love him. As we lay together in that small cramped room, I said that I would be waiting for him and that he was to get word to me somehow.

Chapter 21

Ma Has to Go In

By great good fortune I met Mrs Emilie Kaye who was employed, even as I was, in the Girl's School. She was second in charge at the industrial school in Parramatta where one day, as I was talking about my problems with my Mama, she listened most sympathetically before suggesting a particular home where she could assist me in getting my Ma cared for. It was in Maitland, which meant I would have quite a journey to see her, but she would have devoted care.

She told me that she had heard that a woman, Susannah Rayner, had died in her 74th year of burns, which she had suffered from smoking a pipe that had fallen onto her clothes. She said that she was sure that I would not wish for that to happen to my Ma, so why not take up her suggestion? I realised that she was using this piece of knowledge to influence my decision. I must say though that, even before hearing this I had made up my mind.

Even with her assistance I knew however that it would cost me a mortal mint of money to have her looked after in a manner that I was willing to accept. I could not just have her shut away just because I could not care for her myself. I needed to work. With Jamie the other side of Australia and my husband gone to God knows where, there was only me to provide for the future. It was no use neither thinking of John Adam, he had troubles a-plenty with that wife and no-good artist son.

I looked around for something to sell in our poor quarters. My eye lighted on the wedding present that Pip had given Phillip Gargery and me. Despite its ugliness might it fetch something? I determined to take it into a pawnbrokers shop on the morrow, so having at least some sort of plan I went to bed. I dreamed of Pip saying to me that his present was valuable, so be careful not to drop it. I woke early to hear the birds screaming. I'm usually no believer in dreams, but when I told Ma my dream as we had our morning tea, she said that it was a good omen, and helped me wrap up the china in some old newspaper.

"But be careful, Livvy, those Jews will rob you blind. They have ruined many by their grasping at a profit. And even where there seems to be none, they will contrive to make one. So don't believe a word of what they say."

I promised to be careful. Ma, from whom we had kept Toby's betrayals, then cited him as the sort of decent honest white man that we could trust. She lamented that those Jews weren't more like him. I could have told her the truth, but what was the point?

What a disappointment! A close inspection by the pawnbroker revealed that they were worth very little. Turning from him, I ignored the paltry amount that he was offering, and went to leave the shop. With my hopes raised and now dashed I cried, something that I hadn't done for years. Because I had tears in my eyes I missed the step, stumbled and dropped my hideous china ornaments. When I picked them up they were cracked.

Angry at my clumsiness, I pushed away the pawnbroker, who trying to help me up, said softly and sadly:

""Now, I cannot make even such an offer."

He gathered up the pieces and we both looked at each other for there was more than just broken china. It was something that glinted in the morning sun.

"Mien Gott in Himmel! "

He scrambled to his feet and ran to the door shutting it and turning the sign so that it said 'SHUT'. He bolted it and turned to me.

"All this I do for your safety, dear lady. With these you are now a very rich woman. Only once before have I heard of this. In such a way to smuggle gold from the goldfields was done. These two bars are worth a fortune."

I looked at him, my question unspoken but just as clear as if I shouted it. He smiled sadly.

"To buy from you these I would be needing more money than I have earned in my life. Nu, I give you the name of someone who can buy."

He helped me wrap them in the newspaper. As he did so his smile of pure pleasure at my good fortune was better than the sunshine.

Sitting with Ma in the home, I took her hand in mine and asked:

"What's it like giving birth?"

She began to answer my question then stopped. Looking sharply at me, she frowned, and as I nodded slightly she smiled in delight. We needed to say no more. Now she had something to look forward to, and when in due course I was able put Arthur Phillip John Gargery into her arms her smiles were mixed with tears as she said:

"It's the Magwitch Effect."

I carried on visiting her but she was obviously failing fast, and on some occasions hardly knew me.

I sat with Lizbeth, having come from visiting Ma.

"She's very confused now. She insists that my Pa is coming to see her. She doesn't seem to know me anymore."

Lizbeth got up to put more hot water in the pot.

"She also says that it's the Magwitch effect. I asked her what she meant, but she simply looked past me and said that her Jamie was coming."

"I think that I can tell you what she meant. She told your husband and he told me. It was soon after Pip Pirrip got his inheritance. Your Ma was so pleased she couldn't contain herself; she couldn't wait to tell someone what she thought. As soon as Phillip came home she sat him down and poured him a drink. Then she explained that Abel Magwitch, through his coming to New South Wales has affected a whole group of people; she called it the Magwitch Effect."

The following day when I visited Ma again they said that she had passed on. They added that she was very relaxed, very peaceful at the end. As I left, one of the aboriginal staff stopped me.

"We were very glad he came before she went on her last journey. She waited for him, you know."

I was puzzled.

"Who came? Who was it?"

"Why, her husband, of course. We all saw him."

"You couldn't have. He's been dead for years."

She smiled and put her hand on mine. I felt the warmth of it as she said:

"He was a good man. He helped revenge some of us. He also told us to tell you that you were right about the lamb."

I was staggered. Only my father and I knew about that incident on Amanda Jane's farm.

The end

Those who know about Australia's history will recognise in my book, real people as well as characters that I have imagined. I have taken liberties with these real people and with events in order to tell how transporting a man like Magwitch could have had had lasting effects. Of course, every transported convict has had an effect, some bad, but mostly good. Something that modern Australia is extremely proud of today.

www.ingramcontent.com/pod-product-compliance
Lightning Source LLC
Chambersburg PA
CBHW021955010726
47494CB00003B/749